"Get this extraordinary colle⸺ ⸺ow! They're
worth it! The sensibility is SF, but I wouldn't call them that.
The language is explosive, energetic. You should be in that
armchair, this word-wonder in your hand, reading."

—Samuel R. Delany

"Superbly crafted, *Arkdust* is a harrowing, action-packed,
wildly imaginative collection of stories. More than simply
revealing us to ourselves and warning us of impending
doom, it exposes how there really is no line between the
apocalypse and the now; this is the end and no one told
us--certainly not so creatively. This book is vivid, terrifying,
rebellious, and dazzling. What a fever dream. What a clari-
on call. It will stay with me for a very long time. Alex Smith
is a master storyteller.

—Robert Jones, Jr., author of *The New York Times* bestsell-
ing novel, *The Prophets*

"A sharp sweet hit of the weirdest, hottest drug you ever
took. Every page is splattered with sex and action and heart
and blood and I couldn't f*cking stop reading."

—Sam J. Miller, Nebula-Award-winning author of *Blackfish
City* and *Boys, Beasts and Men*

"*Arkdust* adds the texture and "divine mingle-mangle"
of unapologetically Black and queer lives to vibrant,

Delanyesque speculative fiction, which ranges from super-hero stories to futuristic cyberpunk to experimental weird fiction. Smith's technicolor prose practically jumps off the page, leaving after-images that shiver and glow."

—Craig Laurance Gidney, author of *A Spectral Hue* and *The Nectar of Nightmares (Stories)*

"Alex Smith is criminally slept-on. *Arkdust* explodes onto the scene in a flurry of stardust and cosmic radiation. From time-lost activists to fallen queer superheroes, this book conjures image after image and world after world glowing with energy, humanity, and unmatched vision. The world is a better place because this book, this talent exists!"

– Alex Jennings, author of *The Ballad of Perilous Graves*

ALEX SMITH

ARKDUST

ROSARIUM

For Liz

Rosarium Publishing
P.O. Box 544
Greenbelt, MD 20768-0544

www.rosariumpublishing.com

Contents

The Final Flight of the Unicorn Girl

"We grinned at sin, mostly, spiraling through black ether as a bright yellow wave, crash-landing on the roof or splashing into windows on wires, reeling off one-liners and brash talk that belied the danger of the situation. A flunky with bad breath and an ill-fitting suit would pull some kind of lever, and these hired goons—probably deadbeat fathers with no pension or former mercenaries bored and ill-adapted to civilian life or meatheads spawned from some cult or hate group they'd been kicked out of—would all come trotting out, decorated with surplus pouches and clunky artillery hanging from the taut string of their utility belts.

"We waded across floors riddled with spent shell casings and turned these goons' guns into splinters. We jacked up men in suits, crashed through the skylight in the boardrooms of these shadow corporations; we hemmed mobsters fat with the toxic nuclear steroid of the month to cement walls. Guidos jacked up on super-powered drugs and contaminants, they all flinched and fired aimlessly at our swift, gliding rainbow of dizzy confusion.

"We bounced on drug tables and kicked over artifacts illegally procured from alien worlds in alternate universes. We burned buildings down to the ground, a gleeful flick of a finger on a kerosene-soaked hallway, swept away in the backdraft, watching the flames lick at our winged footies as we blasted back into the night sky. We stood there defiantly in the streets as we razed villain enclaves or looked through high-tech binoculars from a few miles away as one after the other—these towers of oppression—fell from the lines in the sky, crumbling into a pit of ash and mold—just fragments of ideas left, just the rocks. We smiled wildly at the sight, some of us running up light posts and baying at the moon or waving flags bigger than our young bodies, bright crimson drapes of cloth swaying gently in the night breeze, emblazoned with our crests. Or some of us would let loose, wearing jetpacks and bursting out of fireworks and letting the lights entangle us in red stars and green lightning bolts and violet hearts.

"So, don't just let us die out here."

The rain is almost toxic, feels like acid is going to eat through my overcoat. I look at this boy in my arms. He's wearing a silver spandex suit; he's also wearing about seven bullets lodged in places that don't seem to make sense. He's such a lithe thing, just a ragged string, really, tattered and bleeding out in this alley behind this club, one hand holding his guts in and the other raised at an awkward angle toward my stubby face. His touch is like Popsicles on my skin.

"Don't let us die," he squeaks out. His eyes roll up in their sockets, and it seems like he disappears, like his skin tightens right there. I lower him to the ground, gently laying him on a pile of newspapers and trash. I close his eyes and promise him a proper burial, that I'd come back when it's all over and take his body out to sea or scatter his ashes over some great mountain. It's a gentle lie, I think to myself as I clutch my gun, rising to my feet.

There are searchlights overhead. It's heavy and

opaque all over with the radiant stench of D.A.R.K. Patrol's heliports. I make my way up the alley, careful not to cast my shadow in their lights. It's not a lockdown, but I'm trying to keep a low profile. There are too many of them out here.

Something's going down tonight. I can feel it in my gut.

As the last heliport disappears over the bridge, their engines reduced to a safe hum, the streets seem quiet. Hollowed-out sports cars and abandoned motorcycles for blocks; storefronts boarded up and rotting, some still emanating their husky dust and ash, pieces still falling. The occasional vagrant passes by with a shopping cart or something on fire, cackling, then tossing that fiery thing into a bus, a building, or dumpster. The whir of alarms stretch from all angles of the city and lurch down its streets. It's a sound that registers as infinitely more calming than the three seconds of silence before it.

These streets are an abyss, a coiled snake choking itself on the husks of old subway cars, billowing smoke and foul steam cascading its prostitutes; these hustlers stay backlit by a piss-yellow glow of tech-spruced Cadillac headlights. The steady drum and thrum of bass music bursting out of shit-drenched tenements and muscle cars is an unnerving soundtrack. It's giving me a headache. I tuck further into my trench coat, the blood of the silver-clad boy slowly drying on my fingers.

What was his name? Silver Soul? I think. I can't keep all of them straight anymore. No full memories that any of them ever happened. Just bits and pieces like distorted dreams. How they'd streak the air like shooting stars. Back then you could take your child to the park at night and watch them light up, beautiful beacons. We were safe. They kept us.

Yeah, Silver Soul.

He could turn metal into light. He was Captain

Starjack's sidekick. Just this wispy little sprite, flitting in and out of hyperspace. Silver would turn entire tanks into flurries of light ... man, it was something.

On a routine outing, the two of them under attack by some nefarious, now defunct corporation—I'm going to say it was Amnodyne—was when all of this wonder, this dream life we lived traversing the stars only to come spraying back into the atmosphere aglow, anew— all crashed. Amnodyne, we'd all find out later, was somehow controlling the city—its politics, its police officers, its private and public interests. If they didn't control it outright, they owned a heavy controlling interest in it. When Amnodyne's android minions attacked a hostel, laying into a group of boy travelers, Silver Soul saw red and unleashed an array of energies that annihilated a city block. He was inconsolably angry, pulsating with the chroma of the cosmos.

I remember Captain Starjack staring blankly into a news camera at the podium the day that he announced his retirement, that they'd all be retiring, melting back into obscurity, and that some of them, the ones with the real power, would be working for a new corporation that would rise in Amnodyne's wake, take control, and lead us out of the coming darkness. They called it "D.A.R.K. Patrol."

Maximus, Killgirl, Vehenna, White Star, G-Man. They all put on business suits and became the brainwashed henchmen of an international corporation that would strangle the life out of the city it swore to protect.

Where I'm standing isn't the entrance to a club. Not really. It's a boarded-up wall wheat-pasted with wanted posters seeking the capture of Kid Lightning, Girl of Thunder, Hippy John, Coldwave, the Young Arrows Guild, Fangra, Black Bird, Silver Soul. Dead or alive. I touch the boy's face again. On the poster he's glowing, his smile looking sadder now than when that picture was taken.

Some surly young men on junk motorbikes are rolling silently up and down the block. They're waving empty beer bottles around like Molotov cocktails. They've got pig snouts sewn into their flesh with enormous rings or pins made of human bones. The spikes on their jackets have all dulled or chipped away. They're all armed with their square guns and satchel grenades. I try to stay out of the streetlight, just duck into the blackened jamb of a nearby doorway and watch them motor on.

I run my hand, tapping gently on the wall until I find a hollow spot, and bang on it in a deliberate rhythm. Three seconds later, a small hole slides open. Two eyes glare back at me then dart around, widely surveying the surrounding street. They speak. It's a hollow, disinterested timbre. "Go to the alley."

So, another alley. There's a rusting metal door. I bang out the rhythm again, and this time the door creaks open, revealing a blackness that is almost impenetrable. I hug alongside what I think are walls, tracing my path forward with my hands until the walls move, slowly pulling away and rolling like logs down a river. They're not walls anymore. They're people, pulsating and gyrating, clamped to each other in lust. Fucking disgusting. I tear away from them, their bodies slick with sweat.

As the darkness starts to dissipate and morph into a low light, the hallway becomes imbued with a dim redness immersed in a murky underwater glow. The walls turn into glass tanks. Young men and women are swimming nude in a green soup. They are moving in and out of each other's bodies. It makes me dizzy. I finally hear a rumble of bass, a roiling, muddy sound that grows louder as I approach another door. This one is guarded by a big bear of a man. He gives me a nod. I've made it this far, I must be "cool." When he opens the door I'm left standing in Leviticus.

The club isn't massive, but its nondescript outside belies its true size. The music is a dense, thick briar of wiry, disconnected sounds, stabs of half-beats and exploding loops, and a tireless tribal drum. Then there is relentless, merciless, unending bass.

Club Leviticus, the hidden world of decadence, of release. There are bodies everywhere, covered in glitter, shimmering in refracted light. They are swinging on the house lamps; they are hugging the speakers; they are in cages; they are on platforms gyrating in waves. Most of them are young men, barely nineteen, all with a stunned, gray coldness in their eyes, which long to burn, long to find the joy and flame of the heavens again.

I'm at the bar.

"You, there!"

A cackling thing in a pink suit with dull strings of green, red, orange lights piping around the torso haphazardly. She's got a unicorn's horn protruding from her forehead, and she's carrying a ridiculously oversized bottle of malt liquor. "You there, Mr. Trenchcoat! Come to save us all!" she burps out, stumbles through the crowd, and crashes into the stool next to me. Did she pass out?

I look down. She's still moving.

"What do you want?" the bartender, a man with a large head, leathery green skin, and sawed-off horns, asks.

"Nothing." I take another glance at the flesh moving behind me, spitting their drinks back into each other's mouths, grabbing their crotches, or wrapping themselves up in cable wire. "I'm OK."

"Well, you can't sit at the bar if you're not going to order anything," the bartender yells over the music, slamming his huge mitts on the counter.

"Hey, Chang," a voice calls from the other end of the bar. "Relax. He's with me."

A young man with his face buried in a drink gives

me a light nod. Chang turns around in a huff.

The kid, however, just sits there silently through what I perceive to be about two songs. I've got nowhere to be tonight but here. So I sit, too. I finally break and glance over in his direction. The long locks on his head drape over his deep cavern of a face. I can't make out any of his other features, but I lean toward him, and ask, "Are you Coldwave?"

"Ha." He snorts. "Coldwave. Haven't heard that one in awhile." There's another bout of silence from him, then: "Yeah. Yeah, haven't heard that one in awhile, man. What brings you here?"

The boy pulls a flask tucked into his pants, dumps one of the shot glasses in front of him, pours some, and slides it over to me. One sip and my head spins. It feels like I'm watching a really bad home movie on a failing VHS player: my vision is blurry and distorted, and the whole scene warbles in and out of focus. I try to adjust my eyes in the mirror, but all I can see is a young boy running roughshod through a mansion. He's wearing a cape and twirling a staff that seems five feet longer than his body. His exuberance is astonishing as he leaps through the air, over couches, sliding down the length of a dinner table and crashing into book shelves. A hapless staff of maids and butlers cower at the display.

"Scout." A voice, stern and meaty, so clear in my head. The young boy turns around, and a sadness creeps over him. "What is this?"

The man is a square-jawed titan, his chest barreling out of a black Kevlar vest rife with bullet holes and ripped and gashed at the seams. His face is lined with fresh cuts and drying blood. Strangely, he looks a lot like me. He's holding a tattered notebook. He begins to read:

"'Scouts log 22. Today, after patrol, I went to Unicorn Boy's secret, secret Secret Lair. We played video games and talked about our adventures. He has a voice like a thousand gamelans chiming in a soft, sweet rain. So, like, anyway, in the middle of us talking about our battle scars, he took off his shirt to show me one of his, and I touched it, right above his naval, and traced my hand down ...'

"Jesus, I can't even read the rest of this out loud."

The man that looks like a younger, brasher, thinner me stands there, his arms folded.

"You disgust me," he says to the boy. "I want you out of this house by the morning."

He turns away, and the boy sinks to his knees, his long staff falling gracelessly by his side, rolling out into the middle of the floor. The boy cries and cries.

"... don't know anything, man. In fact, I'm not even sure how you got in here—how you even heard about this place—but it's not safe for you here."

Coldwave has been talking for a few minutes. I used to be so astute, my every thought trained on my surroundings. Now I'm 40 pounds heavier with a slumped back, and I'm wearing a trench coat in a seedy nightclub filled with a bunch of mutants and alien freaks, tomboy acrobats and junior assassins with glowing teeth. I've missed out on the drunk ramblings of a desperate teenager who could turn mountains into water vapor.

"See, this is where it all went wrong." Coldwave bangs his glass on the counter. "We got too powerful, man. We always were more powerful than the supers. They couldn't handle it. We were just a buncha rags, just some punks with Day-Glo underwear and pink spandex with our pathetic, little wish powers that we couldn't control.

"But the day Silver exploded, man, that's when it all changed. We started using science to ... to ... to fuel our imagination, right? To get good at using our little joke powers. We started transforming the world, man.

"Sun Runner, who could fucking talk to the sun, ha ha, right? Well, dude figured out how to turn his gift into solar energy, man, and powered all those villages in Africa. Or that dude, Shells from Detroit, who could create those little force fields? Well, he figured out how to use that shit to grow these little bubbles in all the brains of them corrupt politicians, nearly brought the city to its knees.

"Some of us wanted to make a difference, man! And look what they did, used the supers to take us down, stopped returning our phone calls. Now G-Man is working for the pigs in Washington. They forgot where they fucking came from!"

Coldwave downs another, bangs his glass. Chang grunts, then fills it. Another silence.

"So. What are you looking for, anyway, old man? Are you an ex-super trying to relive his sick fantasies all over again, huh? That get you off, old man? You wanna fuck one of us in your big, stupid mansion out there in the 'burbs?"

I want to wretch at the thought. "No," I tell him, reaching into my coat. He flinches, braces himself. I pull out a piece of paper. "I don't know why, but I need to find this person."

I put the paper on the counter, and Coldwave's eyes beam. He crackles alive, his formally sullen face now bursting with a ray of hope.

"But that's ... so you're ..."

A body is tossed into the glass behind Chang. It's the bouncer. He's covered in glass, writhing in pain, lacerated and bloody. The place erupts in startled screams as the unwelcomed hint of danger becomes real. The pig-nosed thugs from the street are inside the club, and they are gunning everyone down. Shards of wood and steel fly savagely around the room.

I'm crouching under the bar, reaching up to pull Coldwave in.

"Fuck yeah!" he screams.

Coldwave slams his glass down onto the table, shattering it. The liquid inside spirals upwards. Before it hits the table, he's turned it into a hundred cold pieces of nitrogen bullets—ice that goes boom—and he's blasted two of the *Mad Max* rejects into a mirrored wall.

But there are three more of them. They have trained their square guns on him. Chang appears from behind the bar and fires an errant shotgun blast. Then his large head explodes into a bloody pulp, the bottles behind him shattering, raining glass and bad alcohol everywhere. In a flash Coldwave is consumed in concussive fire, his body puffs smoke through gaping holes. More guns go off, more bodies fall to the ground in nearly poetic waves of humanity.

Glass canisters of green soup rip open, and fleshy young men pour out of them, choking and gasping for air until they turn into husks.

It's faint, but from my hidden vantage point amid the wail of gunfire, I can hear the gunmen laughing until the table I'm hiding under disappears and their guns are trained on me.

In that split second I see the static memory of a beautiful young boy darting from window to window, running on the rooftops. He's an orange blur twirling a staff—a majorette. He's holding it aloft, and he drops down from a tower into the crime-rich stew of the city, straight toward me, poised to strike. I hear the *click-clack* of a gun trained to fire.

"Scout." I try not to whimper. "Oh, Scout."

When the bang comes, I feel blood trickling in small drops onto my face. And another. *I'm bleeding?* I think. I pat myself, still alive. No, I'm not bleeding. I look up. One of the pig goons has been impaled by a unicorn horn.

The drunk woman, pink suit wrapped in plastic wires, is standing over me. She sinks spike after spike into the three remaining killers. They all go down in a violent heap. When the carnage is over, she wipes her horn with a discarded piece of spandex, fixes her thick dreadlocked mane of hair, and looks at me. She seems to be sobering up quite quickly. I reach up to her, but she just dents her eyebrows toward me, fuming.

"Fuck you," she mutters through gritted teeth. "Just ... you know what? Fuck you."

The other patrons who have survived the onslaught slowly gather themselves, whimpering and cradling each other, shaken with fear. "And you know what else? Fuck THIS!" She kicks one of the bodies of the gang members. "I'm fucking Unicorn Girl! I'm fucking sick of being treated like an anomaly, like hiding in the crevices and existing only in the imagination. I touched the goddamn stars, I made these dark motherfuckers who they are. And you know what? I'm taking this shit back. So fuck you."

"Where are you going?"

She walks back toward me, through the dead bodies, and past the simpering clubgoers.

"I'll tell you where I'm going, asshole," she says to me, two inches from my face, her breath like an acidic onion on fire in a porn theater. "I'm going to walk out that hole in the door and back up to hell. I'm going to dance in a field of space locusts and swim with star dolphins. I'm going to the Nebula Zoo, to the Enchanted Goddamn Forest of the Outraged Mermen. I'm going to barter with ghost Martians at a street bazaar on the hidden moon of Jupiter. I'm going to find G-Man and Maximus and White Star, and I'm going to kick their skulls into a fucking volcano. That's where the fuck I'm going."

She looks at me with an unforgiving fierceness, then her face softens. She tilts her head to the side, and through one solitary, long tear, she touches my face. "I'm going to find Scout, you stupid, useless, bigoted fuck."

But the roof tears off of the club, an implosion like a soundless warp ripping through. Bodies are sucked up through a purple tractor beam and into the air, a rapture of dead and dying lifted into the sky. A heliport hovers ominously, its presence there like a planet's, just pumping gravity by the ton into the atmosphere.

"Attention, Joshua Jones aka Unicorn Boy."

"It's Unicorn Girl, you fucking breeder!"

The swirl of wind and light is great. We are standing there like miniatures of ourselves before this machine, its dark, sprawling technology seemingly blotting out the moon. I can barely feel my legs under me.

"This is G-Man of D.A.R.K. Patrol. You are in violation of Supers Code #DP234. Please come quietly and face trial and subsequent punishment for your crimes."

Suddenly, I remember: I took Scout to a dojo on his first day under my mentorship.

"I thought we'd start on the ground level," I told him, smiling, patting him on the back. He slumped his shoulders, pouted. If he'd had his way, he'd have been turning back flips on the limos of mob bosses and drop kicking tundra barbarians his first night on patrol. I wanted to teach him discipline. What I got was a call from the sensei screaming into the phone, demanding that I pay all of his students' medical bills, repair all of his gym equipment. He barred both of us from the local martial arts community.

When I picked him up from a small village in Viet Nam after leaving him there for a year, he pouted all the way home, listening to Tibetan monks chanting in his headphones while we rode quietly in our private jet. And yeah, it made me sick to my stomach. In fact, it was all I could think about: Scout lying on a cot, wrapped up in the arms of Unicorn Boy, the two of them ... making love on that filthy mattress in some squat somewhere downtown, lost in the gallows of their own desires.

Well, it did then, anyway. But now ... I don't know, I'm looking at him, at her—now, Unicorn Girl, tiny fists clenched and ready, staring into the abysmal shadow of the D.A.R.K. Patrol's heliport.

I straighten my collar, smooth out the edges of my coat, try to stand erect, and I say directly into the purple light, "It's OK, G-Man. I'll take it from here." My voice is deep and resonate. It's a full, square-jawed voice like a radio announcers. "The young lady's with me."

Unicorn Girl turns her head. "You say the dumbest shit, old man," she says to me with a cocky smile.

This is right before her face sinks back into sadness. She's drifting away from me, pulled toward the empty, black hole, lost in the tractor beam's pull, and in a blink ... she's gone.

What We Want, What We Believe

1. We want freedom. We want power to determine the destiny of our Black Community.

Regina Adams let her hair lick her face in the pulsing rain. She ducked under a canopy near Lee's and waited, her body drenched. Working down at the community college during the day, taking classes at night, she was "gonna be somebody," even if the long hours meant she couldn't be somebody's somebody.

A car pulled up to the corner, and a man rolled down the window. One of them long cars, she thinks, used to be white, painted black.

"Who you out here for?" the man asked.

"Excuse me?" Regina said, taken aback. She straightened her knock-off Pierre Cardin skirt, tucked her satchel closer to her body, and shot the man a look.

"Bitch, don't let me get out of this car," the man said in a low tone. His one gold tooth was noticeably dead and dull but still somehow shone in his rear-view mirror as he subtly adjusted himself.

"Who in the car, babe?" Randall, from seemingly out of nowhere, called out as he approached. He called himself Rand X, always reading, hanging with Fives. "What's happening? We having shrimp tonight?"

"Oh, that's your nigger, huh?" the man in the car

said to them.

Rand shot him a look that was all tight-jawed and narrow-eyed, pulling Regina in close. "The lady's with me—" He paused, then, "Rollo. Yeah, I know who you are. And I know you, with your various ... um, entrepreneurial endeavors ... don't have time to mess with decent folks like us. So, if you'll excuse the missus and me ..."

"Hmmph." Rollo leaned back in his seat, tapping on the gas, fixing his bouffant hair in the mirror. "You activist boys." He shook his head. "Ya'll ain't good for business. Consider that a fair warning."

"You have a good day."

Rollo's fake-slick car crept back up the street. Regina, lost in the moment, suddenly tugged wildly away from Rand's grasp. "Boy, if you don't get your hands offa me!" she demanded.

Rand had been trying to talk to her since freshman year. She saw him change from a delinquent kid, a bag boy, a stick-up kid, and petty crimes to a man walking through campus. He was not taking class one, just using the school typewriters to make his little pamphlets.

"Sister, no disrepect, I was just—"

"You were just ...?"

"Tell you what, if you won't let me walk you home, huh, then," he said, handing her a pamphlet. There was a crude drawing of a black panther on it. "Come down to the YMCA on 52nd. There's something going down, and we need all the intelligent sisters like you in the front row. Ya dig?"

Regina pursed her lips together and gently rolled her eyes, crumpling the paper into her satchel. She watched him walk away, dapping and shaking hands with other Black men, tipping an imaginary hat to rain-soaked Black women as he ambled up the street, disappearing into the night.

* * *

"This Maya."

"What kind of name is that? You African?"

Kill him.

Maya sits down on the mattress. She grabs the belt, tying it around her arm, tight. The loop feels like an extension of herself. She holds her hand out impatiently toward one of the boys there. They put the syringe in her hand. The two boys sit beside her on either side, barely men. A husky, ambient debris wafts off the bed; the entire thing is encrusted, peeling just like the room walls, thick with dried blood, burnt yellow with cigarette stains. Roaches scamper at the weight of the young men.

Kill them both.

Maya ignores the young men, swivels to one side and back to the other, avoiding their grabby hands.

"Why she like that, yo? Why she acting like that?"

They don't deserve what you possess.

"Would you just shut! The fuck! Up?!"

Maya rises, stabs one of the boys in the face with the needle. She kicks trash about the room. The other boy searches the mattress, slapping newspapers and condom wrappers into the air. He finds another needle and slowly plunges it into his arm.

"This bitch stabbed me in the eye!"

"Yeah, I seen that."

Something seems to wrap itself around her body, something wispy and shaky, a filament of a thing. It feels cool. It's the drug, she thinks, the come down. She wants the long warm drink of an opiate in her veins.

She sees blood leak from the boy's eye, the other swollen with red tears and anger. He's foaming at the mouth. Maya stares at the door and realizes she has never noticed its dimensions before, that its frame was once a sturdy oak. It's splintered and ripped and vacant now, just a doorway. The hall just a pitch black, never-ending hole that seems to retract from her vision the longer she stares.

Why had she never noticed it before?

Something about ... time?

The piles of newspaper, the rotting clothes, the rusting nails sticking out of the floorboards, and no windows. She has not thought about leaving that place for weeks. Weeks like years folded into her sallow skin.

The feeling over her morphs into something darker. Can she see it? All squiggly lines and rotten, jagged teeth encasing her. It swirls around her, seizes her.

The boy lunges at her. Then the thing evaporates, twisting in the air and materializing in the hallway about ten steps beyond the door as a little white girl in an orange dress floats in the darkness. The dress hovers and curls around the child's body. She steels her face, raises a finger, and motions for Maya to come.

The boy grabs her shoulder.

Maya steps out of the door, can feel her feet beating a path toward the girl. The child's lips draw back like dry sacks. Her eyes sink in. The child's face is all jagged, monstrous teeth.

They don't deserve your skin, they don't deserve your drug.

Maya freezes. Then suddenly she is ripped back into the room by a pair of black hands, back into the sad void of the young man's face screaming hot breath on her cheek.

2. We want full employment for our people.

"Regina. Regina, get up."

A beach in California, maybe. A warm sun, a seagull chimed in the afternoon air, aloft but losing feathers. Regina's dress danced on the breeze, alive. Who is this smallish, dark Black man running, panting his way up the short mounds of sand on this beautiful beach?

"Regina!"

Regina was under a desk. She looked up through the bullet holes in the angled, turned-over table top. She held a double-barreled shotgun in her tiny brown hand. Draped over the desk was Harold Martin and over him was Jerome Pratt. Beside her was a skinny Chinese man with soft doe eyes named Tet Tet, clutching his chest where blood soaked his fingers through the brown fishing vest he seemed to wear every day.

"Regina! Regina, get up!"

She could hear him in her head somewhere, rattling down its labyrinthine caverns, but she couldn't see his face. Regina searched the room. Her senses felt nothing but her own breath.

There. Behind a file cabinet. He was carrying an Ingram Mac-10. *The poor man's Uzi*, she thought to herself, analyzing the gun, proud she got it right. Rand X. When he fired his gun, she knew she got it right. A thundering round ripped through the air.

"Regina, go to the back room, now! Before—"

Bullets tore back at Rand. Was he hit?

Wasn't she just lying there cradled in his strangely terse, yet weirdly doughy arms? Was he not holding her the same way he had done every time? Weren't they snug on the couch, watching Lt. Uhura kiss that white man on *Star Trek*? At a reception after a rally on Temple's campus? He was there, right? When she did her best impression of brother Huey while carrying the new bullhorn she bought on South Street with her financial aid money? When she was putting sandwiches and bananas in grocery bags to give to the neighborhood kids for the Sunday meal programs they started that summer? At the gun range. He was always gripping her up from behind, whispering some mess in her ear, playing all the time. Yeah, she "been read that ridiculous red book, Randall; if you don't get yo ass in this bed I'm gonna show you a red book, sho' you right." The moon hung low in the sky that night, looked like a searchlight in clouds when the smoke from the incense hit it.

"Don't worry about me! You have to get out of here! Go to the safe house!"

Another bang and another bang. Rand spun around with a sharp, contorted jerk. Regina saw his body gracelessly drift toward the floor through the sludge of gravity and time.

"Regina ... please."

She turned toward the side door. It was not the one Rand wanted her to go through. She cocked her shotgun. The *shk-chak* put her mind back on the gun range. That was where he proposed.

The bullets ripped through paper. When they reeled it in, he made a quip about changing all the target outlines for pictures of Commissioner Rizzo. She fingered one of the bullet holes and licked her lips. "Not bad," he said to her.

"Not bad," she smirked. "I'll show you 'not bad.'"

She kicked the door in. A supply closet. A stool. Up on top of the stool and out of the small top window. Could she make it? She rubbed the slight bump of her belly. She would have to. She looked out of the window and into the street. A crowd had gathered a few blocks up. Their nervous anger was trained on the front door of the building Regina was trapped in. Just to the far opposite side of the horde was an alley. A black cat walked spryly through a very small pool of rotting juice from the garbage bins. It arched its back and stretched. It looked free.

27

* * *

The bed, though. That's where %% wants to lie. %% lies on the bed. Not supposed to be on the bed, but it's the best place to look up at the ceiling because the entire room opens up from there, a portal, maybe, where all manner of things can come pouring out.

Things like Bouncy.

Why do I wear a suit? Because I am dignified, you see. I wear a suit because I want to walk into town with a gorgeous woman on my arm, perhaps spin her around in the aisle at Bergdorf and the Goodmans, buy her the finest furs at Macy's, serenade her in the hosiery section at K-Mart. Only the best for her, you understand. The finest silver, the finest gold, and lots and lots of diamonds.

"But you're a bunny."

Tut tut, that's neither hare ... snk snk ... nor there. I am a creature of class. A man of grace. After all we've been through together, surely you can see that?

%% sits up on the bed and sighs, weary of Bouncy's ridiculous proclamations. When Bouncy pushed that third grader into the creek, almost drowning the boy, %% let the rabbit stick around despite the fact that it was %% that got a beating for it. Grandma wore %% out, couldn't sit down for a week, couldn't watch *Fat Albert* at all that year. When Bouncy stole some candy from Mr. Griffin's store, he left %% holding it. A long, hot ride in a policeman's car, another beating, and the hushed, whispered tones in the living room later ... "The boy's got problems for the sho'nuff, Elise. But I don't know what to do with him, my daughter dropped him off, and I ain't seen her since."

"I been reading about all these disorders they be discovering, something about the attention deficit. Maybe he needs some counseling."

"Counseling? Not my blood. Ha ha, you can forget that! Wouldn't hear the end of it from Hattie down at the church."

"Mmm hmm, I know that's right. With her sorry-ass potato salad. Well, it was just a thought."

"Nothing a belt can't fix."

You want to open this, don't you?

Bouncy stands in front of Grandma's dresser like a game show hostess. His fur is matted, an eye dangles sloppily from underneath a patch. His suit, rags. A dirty, white foot pokes through the gaping mouth of his floppy shoe. Still, there is a manic composure about him.

%% stands and pushes Bouncy aside. They aren't even supposed to be in there, not on the bed, not playing around in the dresser again. "Just leave me alone. You're bad news, Bouncy."

Moi? Bad news? Perish the thought. Why, I would ...

Bouncy, stumbling on his messed-up shoe, falls forward, into the dresser. It pops open. %% cranes %%'s neck to peak. A piece of crimson, a snatch of soft, pearly white.

Go on. Go on. Yes.

The room darkens. The rabbit stands in a dim light. Then, by itself, the drawer rumbles open. Soft cotton, wonderful velvet; %%'s grandmother's panties are as exquisite as %%'d imagined them. %% gently runs fingers over the fabrics. The clothes seem to grip %%'s small hands. Soon %% is wrapped up in them, flailing on the bed.

%% has forgotten about Bouncy.

"Bouncy Bunny?" %% calls out. "Come lie on the bed with me. Bouncy?"

%% sits on the edge of the bed and peers over to the darkening corner of the room. There's Bouncy, only under a fading net of light. %% can still see the rabbit's mangy face. A maggot crawls in and out of Bouncy's ear. Bouncy sports as soft a smile as he can muster. He dips in a solemn bow, tips his hat, and fades into the darkness.

3. We want an end to the robbery by the white men and the capitalists of our Black Community.

In a diner in Chelsea, a warbling tune by First Choice clicked on the jukebox with the force of a hammer. It snapped Regina out of her daze. She had been wearing the same sweatshirt and baseball cap for the past two days. All gray, a slate of banality. The crowd was small, but there was indeed a crowd. Customers who seemed more like patients, zombie-like and damaged, as they guzzled coffee and folded newspapers with Regina's face splashed all over them in bold print. There was no rhythm to their movement. The bell over the doorway jarred her each time a new face entered and an old face exited. She was grateful for that wretched bell, though. She didn't want to fall asleep there.

Just waiting for—yes, this woman. A stout, dark-skinned creature with an outdated Madame C.J. Walker perm, long coat, and beads. Not very conspicuous, but they told her that she wouldn't be. Wanted posters be damned.

Regina perked up, her eyes darting savagely under her tinted glasses. The woman passed her table and headed for the lunch counter, then huffed slightly as she read a menu. Regina began to peel herself out of the booth, a difficult feat under the weight of pregnancy.

"Sit," the woman said, irritation in her voice. "And take off those goddamn glasses. You look like a fucking fool."

The woman wouldn't look at her. She just sighed. Regina sighed, too, and took off the glasses.

"Over easy, please. Decaf." The waitress tagged the board with the mysterious perm-wearing woman's order. *I look like a fool?* Regina thought to herself.

"You will go to the address written on the third napkin in the holder in the booth near the door. Yes, I know there's a white family eating there. If you weren't wearing that ridiculous get-up, it would not be a problem to ask for a few napkins, would it?

"Once you're there, you will go to the back door, enter through the kitchen, and go up the stairs to the second-floor bathroom. A tub will be there. It will be filled with warm water, lavender. Rose and lilac petals will steep in the water. Two women will wait for you there, naked. They will rub you with aloe, hum gently. You'll drink the elixir in a vial on the rim of the tub. This will relax you. Don't worry about what's in it. Just do it. You will float there, breathing. It will be painful, but they will be there to ease your pain. Worry not. Your journey begins at 6 o'clock tonight. Take care, silly, restless child."

The coffee grew stale. The eggs waited there in the chilly diner air. Regina just stared at them. A wave of panic rippled through her when the white family nodded and smiled at her as they gathered their things and headed to the door, the children making a racket, the father winking at their waitress, the wife pretending not to see it. There were balled-up napkins on the table. Regina darted over to their table, riffling through their plates.

"Hey! What are you doing over there?! Trying to steal my tips, bitch!"

Regina tucked all the napkins into her sweatshirt, ducking her head. "Fuck your tips."

She tossed another three dollars onto the table. When the door chimed upon her opening it, the sound rattled her bones. She looked up at the bell and wondered if she was just like everybody else coming into this diner on a balmy Tuesday morning, each soul ringing this bell, announcing their presence. *I was in this place*, she reminded herself.

***

4. We want decent housing, fit for shelter of human beings.

"Bitch, yass! Slay, girl, yass!"

Mother sits in "the chair." No one else can sit in Mother's chair. The girls sit on couches. Some sit on folding chairs. Some stand. Not in the chair. They wag fingers in approval. Some snap. Where did she get that glorious blouse, that sheer top billowing way the fuck up around the arms and cutting off right below the tummy, fitting like a glove, over shoulders so broad they could tag in for Atlas himself? The burden they carry, Maya thinks, is no less impossible. But there the bitch go, dancing. She spins around and stops, nearly completing a 180-degree turn, only to complete the rest of her half circle in a slow motion.

Now pose.

A slender Puerto Rican man waves a fan, crosses his legs. He sits beside Mother, speaking to and for her. The girl in the blouse poses, magazine sharp. Her jawline clenches tight, hands on her hips; now those hands are cinching her breasts. Then they are in the air, arms straight, practically walking on air to pull down clouds.

The music stops. Was there music?

Maya looks over to Mother. The crone's hand is raised. All of the girls and all of the boys stop, their faces once jovial, clownish, now stoic and hushed. A pause, then Mother speaks:

"Ten."

You heard her!

The man beside her erupts, his fan flitting wildly across, down, and over his face. The music roars back, a pulsing beat like none Maya had heard before. It

drones, it hypnotizes.
Tens across the board!
Then a new girl dances. Maya watches, wide-eyed. Mother leans into the man beside her and whispers into his ear. The man looks directly at Maya, a face like a joker's, mischievous and determined, and he nods.

5. We want education for our people that exposes the true nature of this decadent American society. We want education that teaches us our true history and our role in the present day society.

Push!! PUSH!!! You can do it! OK, now relax. Relax ... there you go, relax. We got you. We got you. Let the—mmm hmm, let the water ... gently.
It's a ...

* * *

Maya digs her hands in the dirt. The pier is quiet except one sound: Amare's screams. Where are they coming from? Why is she covered in blood? The beautiful dirt ... why is it such a pure thing to her? Why do the caps from Sprite bottles and empty Sanka packets, used condoms, and the sea offer such a perfect potpourri? Why is she drifting here and what is she dreaming of?
Amare screams.
Down, twist, she's giving you banjee!
He watches her twist in the moon's light, covered in the thin haze of that rocky hue, silhouetted against the backdrop of a calm wave. This isn't the beach she'd dream of. This is a stage.
Amare kicks his feet in the sandy earth.
Cunt!
Her faded jean shorts ride up over her milky, golden

thighs. Her cropped t-shirt, once white, stained now. Just a few weeks ago, when she walked in London's Ball, she draped her body in the plastic couture of a replicated Yves Saint-Laurent, carried an umbrella that she tied glow sticks around, and pranced down the tattered floorboards in the basement of an African-American community center. She tried a few new moves that night. Amare was cruel:

Bitch look like she's landing an aeroplane. Chopped!

Maya leaps into the near-dark air. She kisses space. That lone second that she is up there feels like a world being birthed. From her place in the sky, she can see everything: a dog lying by its dying, homeless owner; the dangling neon sign by the Chinese spot where she first met Amare after a heroin-fueled night; the steps to the Sylvia Rivera Community Center downtown with its now crumbling facade girded by steel canopies and littered with junkies. Then she is falling back to the wet earth. A split! She falls onto her back dramatically, her hands pointed as elegantly as the craning neck of a swan.

It's about time, bitch.

"My name is Maya now," she told him then. "My name is Maya."

And like I said, it's about time, bitch.

***

Oh ... oh my god. Maya ... bitch, help!

Amare grasps at his throat. Scaly, flaking, alabaster hands reach over and grab him. They have poles in their hands, swinging violently. *Crack!* On top of Amare's skin. Maya grabs at their sticks, pulling them away. They were alone out here, she thought, where did these men come from? Were they the johns the girls sometimes shared the pier with, businessmen and lawyers unsatisfied at home, on their routine hunt for some dicks to suck, some bodies to feel up, to get their rocks off? Were they pimps? Thugs? Rednecks?

Maya grabs one of them, wraps her hands around his neck, lifts him up into the air. He kicks and struggles. She slams him on the ground head first and drags him out to the sea. A searing hot blow to her head. Then it all goes black.

6. We want all Black men to be exempt from military service.

The filter was overflowing. Hot water blistered on her right hand. The pain snapped her back. The rank smell of stale Robustica coffee, overcooked beans, and cigarettes flooded her senses.

"Shit," she exclaimed. The counter was a mess from the over-pour. She sighed, tossed the filter, poured the grainy brew from the flask into a cup, and served it.

"Turkish coffee!" she exclaimed.

A mousy woman in a turtleneck sweater cupped it as if it was a forbidden elixir and she was dying from some ancient disease.

"There's too many grains in this," the white woman squeaked.

"It's—yeah, it's Turkish coffee."

The two women stared at each other for an eternal three seconds until the white woman turned away and sat back down.

Just clean the counter, Regina. Just clean the counter, make these weird hippie burnouts their coffee, smile at their art that looks like a baby shit itself, laugh at their poetry about their souls burning up in the S&M dungeon of corporate America, and just ... breathe. For your child.

"North Carolina's a long way, isn't it?" the white

man sitting at a table near the window said.

"I'm sorry?" Regina replied, a bit uneasily. "What did you say?"

"Strange place, isn't it?" he said, straightening his glasses. He looked like Clark Kent. That somehow made Regina nervous.

"Duke's Coffee?" Regina asked, throat quavering a bit. "A little. I'm used to it."

"Hm." The man took a sip of his coffee. Did Janice serve him before she clocked out? "I bet you are."

She wanted to ask, "Cracker, do I know you?" Instead, she let a tense line crack her robust lips. Shaking, she went to wash a few dishes. She watched a minute go by on the large clock by the door. She watched the door. 5:30 read the clock. Half hour until Sunday close, a sweet two hours earlier than during the week, but still somehow just as achingly long. She picked up a knife.

"Look at this shit," the man called out from behind a newspaper. The mousy white woman shifted in her seat, buried her face in a *Highlights* magazine. "Listen to this: 'We believe that Black people should not be forced to fight in the military service to defend a racist government that does not protect us. We will not fight and kill other people of color in the world who, like Black people, are being victimized by the white racist government of America' ... blah blah blah ... Can you believe any of this shit?"

The mousy woman had gathered her things and ducked out of the door, an uneasy smile on her face.

"Huh. What's that from?" A wave of calmness brushed over Regina. The man had shown his hand. There was no mystery left. Just her and him.

He folded the newspaper calmly and tucked it into his tan leather satchel. He took his glasses off. "I have a feeling," he said, giving his temples a deep massage. He looked directly at her, locking eyes. Regina clinched her jaw. "I have a feeling you already know where this is from, don't you? It's not exactly esoteric knowledge. I mean, I know this is a small town in good ol' North Carolina, but I bet you've heard of some of these kooks. The Weather Underground. One group calling themselves the—what was it? Symbionese Liberation Army? People like Joanne Chesimard. Geromino Pratt. I know you've heard of them."

"What do you want?" Regina demanded, calmly, raising her voice to crest over his. "I've got—I've got work to do. I got to wrap these croissants."

"I know, I know, I'm sorry," he insisted. "Listen. Here. Here's my card. If you ever want to talk ..." He held the card out toward her, but she stayed there frozen, arms crossed. "I'm not with the FBI. I'm not with the government. I just—I want what's best for you, Regina."

The sound of her name chilled her.

"I'm with an agency that can help you. And your child."

Child. Regina. Child. Regina. Child. Regina.

"We can help you. Our—experiments—with getting people like you—criminals, terrorists— into our deprogramming tanks have been highly successful. We can offer you total immunity with your compliance."

She had been so careful.

She watched the man rise, his coat over his arm, satchel tight across his body.

"And really, Regina, there's nothing to think about. Just—we're trying to help you. If we don't hear from you in 48 hours, we will call the police. It's that simple."

And he left. No "Take care," no scene-sealing quips. He simply left and disappeared down a quaint street where he got into a black car that sat there for a minute before turning onto a windy road through the college campus.

Regina locked the door, ran to a pay phone.

"Now!! Do it now!" she screamed into the phone.

She did not wait for the last bus as she normally would. She ran home, power walked through the white neighborhoods. The moon chased her as the sun disappeared into the seams of dusk.

* * *

"I'm Maya!" she screams.

A tube is in her arm. There's a man in a white lab coat standing at the foot of the bed, reading a chart. Three pairs of black arms are resting on hers.

Mother is in the corner.

The man in the lab coat jumps as Maya stirs awake. "You're awake! Welcome back to the world, Mrs. ..."

"Maya," the black faces belonging to the black hands echo.

"Ms. Maya," the doctor corrects himself. "Sorry, this is—well, it's all new to me." He laughs nervously. "They certainly don't teach this kinda stuff in medical school." He returns to his chart. Brown eyes in a flock of blurry brown faces narrow at him. The brown eyes and brown faces turn back to Maya.

"Where's ... Amare?"

"Amare?" one of them asks. "Girl, who is Amare? You almost died, Miss Thing."

"Why are you always fighting white boys, girl?"

"Amare! How is he?!"

They all look at each other. The girls squint and shake their heads, shrug their shoulders. One of them, an older one, says, "How—how do you know Amare? Skinny Peurto Rican pretty boy? Can vogue for days? Mother, how she know Amare? That was way before your time in this house."

"Where is he?" Maya insists. Her jaw is a swollen,

pulpy mash of flesh and teeth. Cuts lace her forehead. "Where is Amare?"

"Amare—" the older one slowly speaks. "Amare is dead, child. He died of pneumonia two years ago."

7. We want an immediate end to POLICE BRUTALITY and MURDER of Black people.

The door exploded open. Regina rushed from room to room calling out her child's name.

A young woman in a dashiki stood at the kitchen table. "Regina?" she exclaimed. "Regina, I've taken care of it. You're all packed."

"Crystal, I need a car now!"

"Look, OK, you not gon' just come running up in here yelling at me—"

The two women stopped, breathed. A tear flowed down Crystal's eye.

"I'm sorry, Crystal. Where?"

Crystal pointed a shaky finger up the steps. Regina tore up the steps and stopped by the child's room. *So small*, she thought. No time. She ran to her room, searching for her bags. A suitcase— plush with a steel-enforced back and wheels. About yay-high. She tore it open and discarded all of the clothes, wheeled it back to the other room, grabbed the child by the arm, thrust the kid into the suitcase, zipped it up, and climbed out the window. *Crystal*, Regina thought to herself, *you know what to do.*

In the living room downstairs, Crystal lit a match. She shrugged and sniffed through some tears. She watched the flame dance a bit. The small bulb licking the air, longing to touch something, to grow wilder, calmed her a bit. She tossed the match onto an old, ratty couch. It was soon engulfed in flames.

* * *

It's dark. Tight. Every few minutes there's a bump, then a bigger bump. The small bumps go unnoticed. A strong stick pokes through the darkness, pricks the arm. Sounds vibrate through thin canvas walls, filling the air with a redolent creepiness. There are only snatches of them. A chorus of men laughing and sho'nuffing, all muffled bass. A radio buzzing like small insects. A heavy, humming car engine that sometimes sputters, sounding like distant fireworks over a calm field.

%% can breathe through a hole just above %%'s head. If %%'s neck cranes just a tad, %% can see stars flit by in a static kaleidoscope. Suddenly, there's no ground. %% is floating in space, drifting for a second or two, until landing in a huff.

A long stillness. No sound.

Something pokes a tiny hole that reveals the black sky. Something snickers, gnashes quietly, a sound like thin, translucent paper tearing. And then a loud rip and it's as if someone has unzipped the universe and opened up the blackness into another dimension. Standing before %% in a clean, pressed suit, its sparkly eyes gleaming, sunk into its bobbing, fat white head, is a rabbit.

Hey, there.

%% gasps with a start.

Pardon me, lad, yes yes, could you just ... yes, just a bit there.

The rabbit enters into the cramped space, gently pushing %% to one side, and zipping the suitcase back up.

Hi. Bouncey Bunny, esq. It is just ...

The bunny adjusts its bow tie, pats down the suit, checks its pocket watch all while folding itself around time and space ...

Well, it's just fan-tibilly-tastic-a-roonie to finally meet ya!! Heard so much about ya at the ranch!!

... and shakes %%'s hand tremendously.

We are gonna have some fun, aren't we, ol' chum?

8. We want freedom for all Black men held in federal, state, county, and city prisons and jails.

This won't hurt a bit.

Lie back.

Calm.

Nurse?

I know, the needle—she's a big one, heh heh.

Just ... Ms. ... Regina, please. Be calm.

There. There. OK.

See, not so bad. You can rest now.

You know, at the turn of the century, before that even, they considered the slave's ... nurse? Yes, just put it on the desk. Yes, there. Thank you, dear. Where was I? Oh yes, slaves. It was considered a type of pathology for slaves to want to be free. This same diagnosis was first given to women that wanted to, you know, work and not get married. Vote. They called it "hysteria." It's funny how these things become embedded into our everyday society. The same terminology is being used today, except with kids in the inner city. We call it "behavioral issues," or what have you. But really—and this is the sad part—it's all the same. A young Black child isn't a behavior risk just because he, say, doesn't want to sit up in class and listen to a teacher go on and on about great white men conquering the world. He's just acting out an often practiced pathology. He's experiencing and expressing the delusion of freedom. But what is freedom but another boring, earthbound state of mind?

Ah, there. You're almost under. Soon you'll see.

Thank you, Regina. Thank you for coming to see us.

But don't worry. Rest assured, soon we'll find your child. Trust us. Let us nurture you.

* * *

She tucks into her hoodie, hands deep in her pockets. The *City Paper* tornadoes up over a vent bursting with hot air. She kicks a rock with her steel-toe, 16-eye red Doc Martens. It ricochets off of a trash can and onto a parked Buick LeSabre, echoing down the alley. The night is a trapdoor hidden under the moonlight.

Maya pulls the flier out of her pocket. She looks up from the piece of paper toward a heaving, paint-chipped row home. A band is playing. Two white kids in all black, ripped pants, cases of beer in hand, covered in patches adorned with band logos on them, turn the corner, walk up the street, and enter the house. They don't even nod to her. She starts to shake a bit and puts the flier back into her pocket. She searches her memory to make sure—yes, she took her pills today. All of them. She can do this. A woman with pink hair streaks from the house. "Fuck *you*, Gavin!" she screams, throwing a balled-up cigarette pack toward the house.

It's fine. This is fine.

Sighing, Maya enters the house. A thick haze of smoke billows up around her. The din of talk pushing out of maladjusted, pierced white lips is a roar that seems to suck her own thoughts away.

"Check, check," a skinny white boy with a bowl cut of jet-black dyed hair, rocking a white belt, bellows into the mic. "Check. Hello, shitheads. We're Clorox Angels. This is what we sound like."

Roars of guitars and drums topple into each other.

The skinny white boy is writhing like a downed telephone wire. Is there a bassist? It sounds like a drone. *These guys are really good*, Maya thinks.

"Maya!!!"

Suzy's here. She runs up to Maya and hugs her deeply, uncomfortably.

"Suzy," Maya says, her lungs on the verge of collapse. "Hi."

"Oh my god, hi! Maya, are you guys playing tonight?!"

Suzy's enthusiasm is sweet. They'd spent so many hours on top of so many roofs, throwing tiny pebbles at the trolley as it lurched down Baltimore Avenue, so many hours on the bed of some redneck punk's truck talking about Bakunin and dreaming up terrible band ideas, days spent stapling zines and pamphlets before shows only to see them all discarded and lining the floors of the VFW hall they spent all day canvasing.

"We broke up." Suzy tilts her head like a puppy trying to figure out the strange sounds of its owner. Maya ventured to continue over Clorox Angel's cacophony. "How's Eowyn?"

"Oh, you know, screaming, crying, throwing stuff." Suzy shrugs.

"So, she's two."

"Yeah!" Suzy laughs. She has this way of staring at Maya that seems to beg things out of her. Maya has taken to avoiding eye contact, not just with Suzy, but with everyone. Since the pills. They make things better, soothe her. Life on the pills is not just safer, more comforting; it is a lucid dream. Constant work, sure, but easier work.

After the band, Maya sits on the porch. Suzy sits beside her, cautiously. They both stare at the stars. "Thanks for not asking me why I'm at the show and not at home with the kiddo," she says.

"What?"

"Everyone always asks me that. As if it's all my responsibility, you know? I mean, she's got a father, for chrissakes."

"Oh. Yeah, no, fuck that shit." Maya tilts her head down. Suzy edges closer and puts an arm around her, almost knocking her own glasses off. "You deserve a little freedom."

The night is silent. A police car's siren oscillates. Everyone on the porch stops to crane their necks as if they can see the ensuing drama unfold.

"Philly," Suzy says.

"True." Maya stares at the sky, the clouds clearing, welcoming the arrival of a million stars. "Look at 'em all."

At home Maya looks at her pills lined up on her dresser. She takes one and for a moment pretends it's a rocket. The game feels ridiculous and forced, a bit of whimsy that she can't allow herself. But Maya does, eventually that night, take the same bottle of pills and empties it into the toilet.

9. We want all Black people when brought to trial to be tried in court by a jury of their peer group or people from their Black Communities, as defined by the Constitution of the United States.

Curled up on the bed in her cell, Regina, eyes closed, let the atmosphere around her heave against her chest. What a weight. She let her sighs soothe her. The noise of prison rattled around her head. Women arguing over dominoes and illegal card games, cursing out prison guards, shoving and pushing themselves into metal bars at the slightest infraction.

Mostly a low groan and shuffle. The sounds were ambient, snatched samples from dreams. So much so, she didn't hear the noisy clang-clanging of the prison guard's billy club on the cell bars.

"Seventy-one. Get up! You can't stay in here all day!"

Regina rolled over. Her eyes stretched, weary. Her skin was still pulled taut around her frame, still small but lumpy in places. She reluctantly meandered into the television room. The news piped in on the small screen. Gertie was always in front of it, slumped down in her chair backwards, sucking her teeth. The other ladies shuffled in around her. Alice, a simpering white woman who ran her husband over with a minivan after catching him in bed with his step-daughter. Janice, a press secretary for a hedge fund manager caught embezzling investor's money. Rita, a little, rail-thin spike of a thing whose life was a constant whirl of jail, prostitution, and crack cocaine. And there was Regina, ambling around, lifting up books in the library, reading their spines, and putting them back on the shelves. Staring at dust mites or flicking her mashed potatoes with a spoon.

"Something wrong with her," Rita would say.

"Rita." Gertie turned from her TV, so this was serious. "You say that everyday. 'Something wrong with Regina.' Nigga, don't you know we know that? Goddamn." Gertie shot her a look. Rita twittered away, mouthing curses to herself. But never to Gertie. Gertie spun back around. "Dumbass bitch."

"What are you watching? What are they saying?" Alice asked, cutting through the tension with her mewing. It was a way to distract, to get Gertie thinking about television again.

"I'on't know," Gertie shrugged. "But the jawn on here is bangin'! Who is this girl, yo?"

Everyone stopped and peered at the television. They became transfixed, most of them watching for whatever it was they thought Gertie was seeing. They were a throng of orange jumpsuits bent toward the television, hands on hips, arms crossed. All but

Regina who just sat, staring into the void. And Rita, who just stared at Regina from across the room. What was behind those eyes, Regina?

"I don't know," Regina whispered to herself, as if picking up Rita's ambient thoughts through a portal to another plane. All Regina could see was an image of herself in a sundress. She was on a farm. Several men and women in drab gray were clapping, a hardened smile on all of their faces. She walks among them. A man at the end of the line (he looked a little like Clark Kent) held a syringe. A stocky, compact, dark Black man was running straight toward her. He burst through the line of gray-clad clappers, reaches out to her. Everything slowed down. Stopped, rewound. This was it, this was all she saw. "Every bit of my memory is a soup."

Rita snaked her way through the crowd of women in the cell. All of them were watching a woman at a podium. They all thought the speaker was a bad ass. Perhaps Rita did, too. Her curiosity for Regina's truth lured her. Besides, Rita had seen so many "bad ass girls" doing "bad ass things" get cut down by salivating, slovenly, ferocious men, all starved for the attention they drained from their mothers, never got from their fathers, and they now demanded from the rest of the world. Rita will not be fooled.

She sat beside Regina and stared with a child's eagerness at the woman. "Who are you, girl? What are you doing in here?"

The only thing Regina could think to say was, "When in the course of human events it becomes necessary for one people to dissolve the political bonds that have connected them with another and to assume among the powers of the earth."

Rita sat back, stunned. "Look at god," she whispered. "Won't he do it? I knew there was something wild about you! You're—"

"Regina!" Gertie was standing up. Regina reflexively snapped her head toward Gertie's thunder clap of a voice. "Regina, this bitch just said your name, girl!"

Regina pushed through the crowd ... on the farm. The hands clapping in gray are now hands tucked under orange. White hands. Black hands. She moved toward Gertie, who stepped aside humbly. Gertie knew.

On the screen a beautiful woman stood encircled by microphones. Cameras flashed. The woman was tall and lithe with glowing brown skin. Her hair a wild frizz of curls and locks that seemed to flow elegantly. Her stance was of an oak's. She spoke as if words were small fires. "And we will not stop until she is free! Until Leonard Peltier is free! Until Mumia Abu-Jamal is free! Until Geronimo Pratt is free! Until all prison walls are razed! We will not stop! No justice! No peace! Free all prisoners!"

There was something oddly familiar about her to Regina, something in the head tilt, the slight twist of the body. The way her eyes blinked in a staccato rhythm. What was she saying? Oh ... the eyes. The woman on the television, her eyes onyx stones, inky black. They swam in the milk of their cornea. Regina clutched her hands to her chest and let the tears fall gracelessly down her cheek. She waved to the girl on the television.

"That's my ..." Regina began. She paused, squinting, gently nodding. "Yeah, that's my daughter."

* * *

Minutes after she inserts the disk, Maya gets a ping on her computer.

You've got mail.

She's not supposed to be using the office after hours, not after they found her printing 300 copies of a zine about racism in the west Philly Marxist knitting circle community. Not after she let a few homeless queer boys sleep there for three weeks during a particularly harsh February.

She checks the screen.

I have the information you seek.

A clap of thunder erupts outside of the window. She watches Cary, the new programming director, smiling with her precious latte in hand, laughing up the street, clutching a designer briefcase. There are two white men in Birkenstocks standing with Cary, holding newspapers over their heads. That doesn't give them much shelter, but those men think they're bulletproof, that their every machination, every whim, every grant, every invasive design they've hinged the city on, matters. A little rain? They're not impervious, simply unconcerned. It's all Maya can do not to toss the computer out of the window and down onto the street at them.

Don't do that. You'll never find out.

Maya scoffs at the little white text box on her screen. "What makes you think I want what you have? How do I know it's authentic?"

How?

"Yes. How? I mean, you contact me literally two days after I left the psych ward. Days after a Chinese man in a Buddhist's robe passing out tai chi pamphlets gave me—me, specifically—one of these weird AOL disks."

No need for exposition. I know the story.

"Don't get smart." Maya tears open a bag of chips and angrily pops one in her mouth.

Have I steered you wrong before? I told you exactly where the most strategic exits were during the RNC. I helped you and your comrades avoid capture. I told you Dominic was a saboteur working for the Philadelphia Police Department. Everything I've shown you has been real.

Maya bangs furiously onto her keyboard. "And

everything you showed me had a catch. I always had to do some fucked-up, meaningless task before you gave me the full story."

Nothing is meaningless. Nothing has meaning. All things simply are.

"Whatever." Maya flashes the computer screen the middle finger. "The point is, now you're just offering this information freely?"

Yes.

"I don't think so."

Maya, it's true. I know who and where your mother is. It is imperative that you go to her now. It is imperative that you know.

"Bullshit! Prove it."

Another clap of thunder. The lights shutter off. The smell of ozone coats the air. Maya is illuminated by the glow of the computer screen. She feels something gingerly walking up her spine, something pulling tight, yet somehow loose. Not there, but ever present. It feels like woven gossamer. Then it passes.

A buzz and a whir that sound—feel—like a cyborg's death rattle. Maya looks around the room, sure she'd turned all the computers off for the day. It's the fax machine roaring to life. An image takes shape on the page. An arrangement of pixelated characters, letters, and numbers forming odd shapes, each line breaking into rounded pictures, something like a paw, a body, then long, pointing ears.

A rabbit.

10. We want land, bread, housing, education, clothing, justice, and peace.

The island was a strange place.

Baboons would come and steal fruit from their

tables. There was plenty, though. Regina stood under a canopy where she took hold of a large knife—swatting at birds, swatting at monkeys—to cut a pineapple. She put the knife down and ate the succulent pieces of the thorny fruit.

Children—so many children—ran about, playing on plastic motorbikes that cut new paths into the sandy dirt. Regina wondered what kind of danger they would be in, but these children seemed feral, free. She never knew that kind of freedom. Maybe this was just how kids were now. *The internet is making them crazy*, she thought.

People buzzed along on small discs, cutting through the sky while tapping on invisible screens in the air. Diagrams and images appeared in front of them as they navigated over the water, down the beach, through the trees.

A Black man in a long, flowing robe held hands with another man, brown-skinned and shaggy haired. They pulled each other close. Their blithe laughter echoed.

Regina stepped out from under the canopy and into the sun. The woman tried to act like she belonged there, absorbing the giant radiant yellow sphere's rays, letting it swim up the canals of her melanin.

Maybe I'll write a poem today, she thought.

She took another step and almost forgot she was standing on an embankment. Whoops! She looked down and a tall, golden, sun-stroked woman with a wild mane of hair was walking toward her in the distance.

She was flanked by two, well-built men, shirtless in flowing pants. One carried a spear, the other typed diligently with one finger on an invisible pad. The woman smiled shyly, stopped, and waved at Regina.

Regina slowly waved back, shaking her head in awe.

* * *

Don't be afraid. They're yours. These are your dreams. I know you want land and bread and freedom and peace. I know you've been through the wars, you've seen the shuttering of shelter, you've looked through the raw-ripped tapestry of the world that was supposed to protect you, and it rocked you, I know. We've always been here, though, with you. It's OK, it's OK. You don't need them. We're right here for you. Always.

Let us in.

We know.

When you put those dreams on hold for this world, when you burrowed through the fog of time, when you screamed into the vortex.

You did, you took those pills to drown us out. You didn't know that we were looking over you, that you're an ethereal being in a corporeal world, a world that doesn't quite understand you. But it's time. We've got you, sit with us.

Wake up now. Let us in.

Maya wakes up. Mother is there. She crosses the room.

"You slept again."

"Yeah." Maya shifts on the floor. Her legs are crossed and numbed. The pain doesn't wash over her so much as it just mists. She's used to it now.

"Get up." Mother's hands are crossed. She is draped in a heavy robe of colors that swirl in shimmering chroma. Her every movement is both grand and effortless.

"It's weird hearing you speak," Maya mumbles.

"The little orphan girl. All grown up." Mother paces. "Came to me as a seed, and now," she says, gesturing. "Look at you. A prickly pine tree? Or a great, big ol' oak?"

"You know I don't do well with this esoteric stuff, Mother."

51

Mother moves so swiftly that it's as if she simply materialized in front of Maya. Mother frowns at what she sees.

"Why can't you see it, girl?" Mother urges, placing her bony hand on Maya's forehead. "Why can't you wake. The fuck. Up?"

A searing heat as Mother pushes down on Maya's head. Steam emits from her hand. Maya wants to scream, but when she opens her mouth there's only a click. A silent, burning, inward scream. A white hot everything.

The light is massive, weighty. There she is, floating in the middle of it. Is this the sun?

The sun, where it all flashes harsh rays, hues of gray silhouettes acting out before her. Her birth mother tossing her into a suitcase. Her in her grandma's clothing, bounding out of a window as the old woman bursts after her, swinging a belt from her bad hip. A night under the pier in solitude, a plastic bag squeezed into a drug kit, tucked under a spoon. A nightclub's dizzying strobe lights and thumping bass. A peer group session at the youth center, tossing a kickball back and forth with other kids in shoplifted JNCOs. A shitty job at Rainbow selling biker shorts to thotty Latinas in the Northeast.

Kissing Suzy on the beach. Starting a band. The co-op, a cop's baton, throwing a computer out of the non-profit's window, watching the shards splash in front of Cary's smug face, bits of screen embedded in the donor she's coddling's foot. A bullhorn. A fire. Walls of a prison crumbling into dust, barbed wire choking a police officer acquitted of killing a Black teen on a playground in Tennessee.

An edict. A convergence of scientists, engineers, eco-ists, fashionistas, and vigilantes, their afros and dreads and box braids resting like impenetrable crowns on their Black heads. A cloud. Maya is floating there like an ... angel?

A hadron collider.

A masked group of men surrounds a miniature hadron collider pulled out of its cryo-cell by barefoot African children riding hyenas through the hallways of NASA. *What*, she asks herself as the heat intensifies and the flashes grow larger, *is a hadron collider?*

Her Mother. No, her *mother*, Regina.

Wearing a black beret. A dashiki. An apron. A gray sweatshirt. An orange jumpsuit. Her mother wrapped in needled-threaded linen adorned with paper-thin golden embellishments and cast in a wreath of doves.

Let us in.

Maya falls back. The light snaps off like a valve shut tight. Maya pants, her eyes darting violently.

Mother stands above her.

"Again," Maya gasps. Her throat is a scratchy, mealy gullet. "Again!"

Mother bends down and smirks at her.

"No," she says, intently. She claps her hands twice, then exits the room through a door Maya did not know existed. "Tomorrow we really start."

Maya slumps to the floor, crying. Her sobs can't be controlled. They ebb, rise, and ebb again, until they become simple breath. She closes her eyes to sleep.

Let us in.

ALEX SMITH

These Are Things That Bad Men
Hear at Night

Clouds burst forth, thick, black piles of steam and soot daubing the low-hung evening sky with their inky lacquer. Even blacker, sootier, rising from the pale green leaves of the tobacco fields was a fine stream of smoke from the fire the hands had set. Carlos, Rafael, and Milo were warming themselves in a hollow. Their shadows bounced around the glow of the blaze like early cartoons riding crossed-up lasers. They were talking about high school baseball and beer, dreaming up tales about women. Sometimes their stories would fall into this uneven amalgam of the three where they would collide and spin into grander fantasy.

Wind licked at their palms. Milo had forgotten his gloves again. His skin—like the tusks of a razorback—white and dotted with blood under its surface—was cracking. Carlos derided him in broken English: *You no like it's too cold?* He tapped himself on the head and grinned a seventeen-tooth smile as if to say, "You dummy." Then he looked at Rafael, who had suddenly grown sullen at the thought of making fun of Milo again. *Let's just talk about beer*, his low grunts said. Carlos cackled, and Milo, through the thick maze of his blood-red beard, turned up his lip and squinted in Carlos' direction.

"Shh." Rafael, squat and bullish, put a finger in

54

the air. Something was shifting in the wind. The soft sounds of leaves rustling were clashing with crisp breakings that ramped through the air with the rhythm of awkward footsteps. They each shifted a degree, casting glances into the dark, hoping the fire's light would aid them. Nothing visible registered. Milo, a sturdy husk of a man, grabbed his knife.

Their lives had been dashed and dotted with episodes of tragedy. For Milo, seeing his family killed in an arson fire set by gangs sent him over the edge. Carlos, a former thief from Colombia who'd escaped two prisons on his journey to America, thought his life as a scraper had ended here on the dust-strewn path that led to the tiny shack he shared with his fellow nomadic field hands.

And there was Rafael. Stout, short, wild-haired, quiet, and sage beyond his years. He had killed a man. In a fit of passion in a Mexican town off the map against veiled advances, he struck out, drunk and wild, and punched and punched until another man's face was a warm, pulpy stain and his bones were crumbly ash.

These were men of violence.

Rafael stepped forward and put his hand on Milo's wrist, holding it tightly. The farmer's son was known to play in the fields at all hours of the day. Rafael had once seen the kid on the hill by the stream that ran just outside of the farmer's territory. He'd been gathering some wood when he heard the young boy, gangly and weird with skin the color of deep, varnished wood, hair stringy and twisted into thin, rubbery locks, talking to himself. It was a strange conversation; part in English, part in a low, gnarled growl that sounded inhuman, almost ... dead? He was throwing rocks into the stream, violently, asking, "This one?" then replying "No," smashing the rock hard against the surface of the water as if to break it.

Rafael had dropped his pile of sticks. With an awkward twist of his head, the boy turned and looked straight at him. The boy's eyes were glassy, and for a moment (perhaps Rafael had imagined it) those eyes were glowing.

"You OK, my friend?" Rafael offered.

The child fell to the ground, shuddered, and screamed, "Go away!"

He did go and left the boy alone to cry until his father called him for supper.

So Milo eased up. His hand was still on his knife. He rarely let men touch him without there being consequences, but now he was almost comforted by it. It felt strange to Milo to have a friend, especially one whose skin was as dust brown and hair as thick as Rafael's.

Carlos was fidgeting by the fire, mumbling to himself in Spanish. His knife was drawn.

The rustling stopped. From behind a row of leaves, crows shot up and scattered into the night. In the stillness about twenty feet away, a man stood on the edge of the tiny, cleared piece of land in the middle of the tobacco field. His eyes were glossed over white. They seemed to explode out of his black face, two moons swirling through space. His teeth were clenched and snarling. Drool trickled over his chin. He was nearly naked, only a pair of tattered jeans clung to his body, his muscles glistening with sweat in the cool air.

The men felt their bodies become slack. They were looking at Tony, one of the Jenkins boys who had come over from a neighboring farm to help with the last of the harvest. They had always pitied him because, although he was adept at baling and weeding and could lug equipment it would take even the best of them to carry in pairs, Tony's intellectual capacity got nowhere near such feats. The farmer simply called him "The Dummy."

Rafael approached Tony, calling his name. The swirl of crows grew denser, louder. Carlos was back to freaking out, tearing a path through the rest of the field with such velocity the others barely had time to notice.

"Tone?" Rafael called and called, each time softer than the first. He touched the rabid-looking man who stood there, fixed. Tony's skin was soft, almost gooey. It made Rafael recoil, which brought Milo's knife to the front.

Tony's eyes rolled upwards. With mouth agape his body sank to its knees and fell to the ground with a thud. Rafael took Milo's knife out of his hand. He poked the fallen man with the blunt end. No movement. No rising of the chest in a slow, but assuring breath. The Dummy was dead.

***

The porch door swung open. The boy looked out onto the horizon. He sat naked in his mother's old chair, careful to keep his feet from touching the good rug underneath the coffee table. He was growing anxious. Every time the door banged against the jamb he would jump. His mind was full of the kind of chaos that wouldn't allow for daydreams. Instead, he sat in his mother's chair, his eyes trained on the porno magazine he had stolen a few days ago from Clegghorn's gas station up the road. It was absolutely thrilling him.

After watching a truck full of farm hands disappear over the horizon, he had wandered after them up the winding dirt road toward town, barefoot and ashy legged. He didn't think he would find any of them at Clegghorn's. Not Milo, the red giant from the Northeast, who he would bombard with a million questions about shooting guns or driving or fixing a car when all Milo wanted to do was finish his crossword puzzle or watch the game and have a beer and fall asleep. He hadn't expected to find Carlos the twitcher picking through racks for his beloved Slim Jims, singing noteless cumbias to himself and pining for women he'd never actually been with. Nor any of the sweaty, dirty men who peopled his father's farm at Clegghorn's that day. He was on foot. They were in the truck.

Least of all did he expect to see Rafael. But when he appeared from the bathroom and caught the boy taking the magazine from the rack and stuffing it down his pants, blood seemed to leave his body. Rafael never told a soul. Because of this, he had emerged as the boy's favorite.

As the wind picked up around the house, he sat in the darkness and jacked off to the pictures of naked women and men in garish positions, fucking lustfully. He preferred the pages that seemed super-imposed from films, where two, three, or four partners were entwined in animalistic fervor. Pictures of women sprawled over the hoods of Corvettes or putting fruit into their vaginas did nothing for him.

He loved the danger of jacking off in his mother's old chair, losing himself in reverie with the pulsating fear of being caught swimming in his consciousness. As he held his penis in his hand, he felt something like fur creep over his thigh. It was a crawling, spidery movement brushing over him, then suddenly a wetness. He wanted to spring to his feet, but whatever it was holding him so gently, so firmly, there on the seat had other ideas. A low, nasty guttural voice spoke.

"NO. YOU WILL SSSTAY, WON'T YOU? WONT YOU?" it demanded.

He whimpered and sobbed. "Yes."

Outside, the wind had stopped. It was like someone

closing the door on a centrifuge; no clanging porch door, no flap of birds. Just the soft rustling of gravel being moved by boots. He looked toward the door.

A shadow moved up the porch steps, but nary a body materialized. He looked back toward his own heaving thighs, where the spidery hands now held him firmly.

"CONTINUE. CONTINUE!"

He didn't even feel himself struck, but a wound opened up on his face and then another on his arms. Blood coated his skin to form a perfect mahogany. He was naked, and his father was walking up the steps.

"Son?"

He was afraid of his dad beyond the kind of fear that any father worth a damn could muster. He'd seen his father kill chickens with his bare hands, turn grown men into simpering pools, and keep a pack of wild dogs at bay with only a stare. His father's thick face was encrusted with deep craters. Dry ridges of skin ran in dunes up and around his lips and eyes. His hair was like barbed mesh and could never stay combed, though he tried. The farmer spent hours in front of a mirror, shaving and pruning his hair, but could never keep it from growing into micro-shrubs of thick wool.

The boy would stand in the hallway and peer into the bathroom while his father shaved and lectured and opined. He couldn't stand still sometimes out there in the cold, dark shaft of the hallway. While his father prided himself on having a son who was silent and obedient, the boy grew more restless. Broiling inside of him was an energy that longed to be expelled. There were straps built into his bed, weights tied to his ankles.

He was made to drink strange cocktails every Sunday before church. The boy lost himself in a haze during service as the pastor's voice buoyed around in his head, the glib timbre of the organ playing a dirge.

The swaying and moaning bodies of the churchgoers around him made him sick. They all sounded and looked like dead souls reaching out of the abyss. One time Annie Mae Glass had touched his thigh and squeezed so hard during her "Amen"s that the ends of her false nails drew blood. Through the drugs he pursed his lips at her, and said, "Fuck you."

The church stopped moaning and moving. Annie Mae fainted and convulsed into a spasm, losing her wig and calling out to the Lord, Jehovah, and Yahweh in all his names.

When they got home, after a long, silent ride in the church van where all of the farmhands piled into the backseat, his father beat him mercilessly until Rafael and another hand cautiously intervened. For his service to the boy, the farmhand was kicked in the shins. The boy was dunked head first into the bath tub and then tied to a bedpost for the night. When the farmer was done he came downstairs and watched the men saunter off to their quarters. He called them from the porch. When they turned to see exactly what it was he wanted from them, the farmer raised a dirty finger to his lips.

That was the night that it first came for him. At first it was a hissing mass of piss and cum on the floor by the boy's bedpost. It evolved throughout the night, grew limbs and a face, sprouted troll hair, and oozed green sludge from its orifices. It stared at him, licked him, and cradled the boy's head in its still growing, pus-filled arms. It leaned in, its tongue and teeth grazing the boy's ear.

"THEY. ARE. ALL. GODLESSSS."

The boy felt his own voice saying the same words, moving through his own mouth as the trollish thing spoke, seemingly giving a plump and pleasant life to the boy's weak lips. When the troll bit his neck he fell asleep, watching the creature tear through his room in a haunting dance replete with jerks and contortions like a flickering newsreel at the end of its tape.

A gentle rain was coming down now. Rafael had tried reviving Tony, had all but given him mouth-to-mouth. He knelt beside him, short of breath, careful not to put too much of his ample weight on his bad right knee. Milo stood over the two of them. He was backing away, trying to figure out what the fuck was going on. This isn't what he'd signed up for.

Milo and Carlos had arrived on the farm on the same day, both recommended by Doc Flanagan from a couple towns over. Milo was making his way back up north and had stopped to make a few dollars to have some spending money. He didn't like Carlos. Thought he smelled, sure, but mostly hated that he reeked of opportunism.

The two of them stayed in the same cabin but rarely slept. Instead, they'd regale each other with one sordid tale after the other. They fell asleep clutching their knives with the sound of the other's voice beating on their eardrums like a chaotic lullaby.

Milo had seen the farmer at his worst, but he, for some unknown reason, seemed to quietly understand, to almost respect the old man. Many nights the big, ruddy man would be awakened, feeling shadows surrounding him. A tiny bit of light spraying into the cabin window and something moving past it. Milo would check, but no one would be there. In a fit of curiosity, Milo asked the farmer one night, "Is this place haunted?"

The man stopped drinking his wine and turned to a slightly disheveled Milo standing in the doorway. The farmer's son was sitting on the floor reading, and without looking up at either of them, the boy grinned a wide, toothy smile so deranged it almost made Milo throw up. The farmer had not noticed. "No," he replied. "Why do you ask?"

A pause.

Milo shrugged. He felt stupid now. The boy's grin had dissolved, and it felt as though Milo had imagined even that.

"It's probably those damn Jenkins boys. They are always fuckin' with the plowing equipment. Nothing to get all worked up about."

Milo watched the boy scamper away, humming a tuneless song like a deranged nursery rhyme. Choking down spit, Milo tried to push the bad thoughts out of his mind and acquiesced, announcing almost breathlessly, "True."

The night Tony died, it wasn't the Jenkins boys who'd done it. They would not have killed one of their own. Who the fuck was out there? Where's my knife?

"Rafael!"

Milo suddenly realized he had backed away about fifteen feet. All the breath in his body stopped. He gagged and groped at his throat.

He saw Rafael try to lift himself up and run after him, but something was dragging him away faster than Rafael could run. Milo's enormous frame flailed wildly, crashing to the ground, still kicking his limbs and grasping at whatever had his throat.

It felt like a thin wire, but it had unbelievable strength behind it. All he could see were the stars. He could feel his head dragging the ground as rocks and twigs dug into his scalp. He could see the stars moving like fireflies in twilight.

Rafael was running through the foliage. He was panting. He kept a steady pace, watching out for movement, stopping to assess things. Should he call out for Milo or Carlos? For the farmer or his son? For any of the Jenkins boys?

He decided he would sit and wait on the edge of the field where the crops had grown largest and he could have a good look at the house hidden by the giant, husky leaves of the dense field. Nothing moved except the darkness creeping around the house.

From a crouch Rafael saw the porch light flicker off and on. When the light popped back on, a man was standing on the porch, his body hunched as if he were dragging something behind him. A sudden gust whipped the door open and slammed it shut.

Clang! Clang!

The light—*spack!*—went out again. Rafael could not see anyone or anything on the porch at that moment. The boy, he thought, was in the house. The same boy, the farmer's son, all of thirteen, who had opened the door on Rafael the day he was in the house bathing.

He had rarely used the bathroom in the house, preferring to wash, shit, and shave in the outdoor facilities. It was good to be a part of nature, Rafael told himself; good to be apart from a civilization that had marginalized him all his life. He could be free out here, own his own body, and let the water and air wash him, dry him, keep him safe. But there were too many men in the field that day, and the farmer was at market, selling and conning all the local distributors. A quick splash in the tub would be fine, in and out, no worries.

He had found himself immersed in the dreamworld of that oversized bathroom, sunk low and deep in the water, steam rising over him and beating the knots out of his flesh. He heard the floorboard squeak. His eyes tore open, and he leaped up, grabbing for a towel and covering himself.

Had the farmer come home early?

No, the boy was standing there with an inquisitive visage, tilting his head to the side, seemingly admiring Rafael's body. When the boy reached up and touched Rafael's penis, the man jumped back onto his bad knee and nearly lost his balance. The kid turned and ran, mortified that he could not control his impulse. Rafael would pleasure himself later that night, thinking of the youngster's cold flesh against his. It was the first such thoughts Rafael had had in a long while.

Another scream tore through the night sky, this one higher in pitch, more frantic. Rafael searched the ground for a weapon, then remembered the knife. He sprang to his feet, running, and took a giant leap over the steps, flung his stocky body over the porch landing, and crashed into the door. The knife squirted out of his hand and slid across the floor.

"Fuck!" he yelled, wincing and clutching his bad knee.

He heard stumbling and muffled crashes reverberating through the walls of the house. It jarred him back to the task at hand.

Get to your feet, he thought.

And he did. He threw his fists up and squared himself, but the only body there was something that looked like a slab of a human sitting on the good rug in the middle of the floor, its back turned toward him. The thing had stringy hair, disgusting welts, and pus-filled pores everywhere.

Rafael's curiosity got the best of him. He touched it. It turned around, its flesh hissing and oozing.

"YOU'VE. COME."

It seemed to speak without moving anything that could be construed as lips. Rafael fell sickly pale and watched it turn into a gelatinous puddle.

"I. KNEW. IT. WOULD. BE. YOU."

It bellowed into the cold, open room, down the hollow hallway, through the walls, out into the fields, down the dusty path, and into the night.

Galactic

I.

They're coming. A sad, beautiful beach lit by sun reflecting on sand. Casper runs his feet under the cool water, the foam licking between his toes in gracious laps. He stares up at the big, round orange hole in the sky. *They're coming, and I'm not ready*.

Malik is standing in front of him. "Hi."

"Move, you're blocking the sun." Casper puts his hand up to Malik's bony chest, gently pushes him to the side. He breathes deeply and welcomes the sun's rays deep into his chest.

"I'm bored," Malik huffs, dramatically collapsing to the sandy floor. "Take me somewhere."

Instinctively, Casper reaches over and gently rubs Malik's side down to his stomach, stopping at the wire of a black thong, slowly working his finger under his bathing suit. Casper's still staring at the sun. "Where do you want to go?"

A phone rings. A gull lands on a rock just a few feet away, fluffs its wings. It turns on its spindly feet and raises its beak at the two men. It lets out a squawk and a stream of white shit.

"Hello?" Malik picks Casper's meaty hand off of his crotch, flings the hand, and then rolls over on his side. "Hmmph."

The sun is a distant citrus dream in a tangle of cloud string. Casper taps Malik on the side, points toward it. "Look." Malik doesn't look. He just sulks.

Casper's on the phone. "Yes, what's up? Where are you guys? No. No. We're on the beach."

Soon the sun disappears. Waves of purple and black wash over the beach, folding into a final, gestating gray. With a chill crawling up his spine, Malik turns toward Casper and buries his face in his shoulder. The seagull launches into the air and is lost in a flock.

"Who is that on the phone?"

"Yeah?" Casper sits up. The immersive gray and then a cloud or two, the fading sun; so sudden. "We were just about to leave."

II.

On Roa, they mined precious stones and forged crystal sieves. There was a great dance before they sent the men into the mines, a dance that shook shackles. They fashioned metal plaques and tied them to ghosts in rituals that burned their cages. Roans went to the highest mountains and started their soul dance at the peak, spinning and twirling there until the sky reached its darkened climax. Little volcanic fissures in Roa's surface emitted fine mists. Men walked through this crystalline spray, one by one, toward their birthright.

"Roth. Get up." Ragolos looked into the bamboo tent. His son was sleeping on a bed of grass. "Get up. It's time."

Without any real protest young Roth gathered at the edge of a long path. Saba was there with him, three boys down the line. They looked at each other. Saba was trembling, his upper lip bouncing furiously into his lower teeth.

Roth closed his eyes and tried to imagine he and Saba running across quiet plains and chasing mup bugs, tying twine to the spindly creatures' enormous tails and sailing them like sentient kites through the meadow as Roa's two suns beat down on their bare skins. He tried to remember sneaking into the temples and stealing jewels, angering the monks who chased them with sticks.

As Saba's simpering got louder, the memory of Roth fighting back a horde of boys tossing rocks at the two of them swelled in his mind. The largest boy in that mob, Staen, put down his rocks, walked up to Saba, grabbed his grass-woven shirt, and shoved him into the dirt. When Roth stepped in to defend his friend, Staen and the other boys beat him to a pulp. One punch lifted him off his feet, sending him backward and landing on the rocky ground. Though Roth's eyes were coated with wetness, each fist pounding him further into a haze, he could still see Saba's feet treading through the grass, getting smaller and smaller and disappearing over the horizon.

Staen was in the line of boys. He was smirking as usual, fighting to withhold a laugh. They all stood there naked, their tar-black bodies exposed. On one side of them, a line of chanting warriors; on the other, a line of humble, broken-bodied men from the mines. In front of them, the monks, praetors, and scholars walked slowly, deliberately, casting flowers and lighting incense as they moved down the path. The village women looked out of their hut windows, their day in the fields, on the hunting grounds, or cleaning the vast libraries, sanatoriums, and monuments on hold.

"Boys!" a praetor announced. "Today you will walk through the mist and emerge a warrior, a miner, a monk! Today you will be shown your destiny!"

A roar from the crowd. Birds lifted to the sky. All of

the naked boys in a hushed silence tensed. Behind the monks in front of them, a geyser of thick red mist shot up. The crowd silenced.

"Come!" shouted the praetor, raising his skinny arms through voluminous robes. "Come and meet your destiny!"

As the monks parted, the boys walked down the line and into the mist. Soon they would emerge with the distinguishing marks that chose their fate. Inside the mist Roth felt searing heat. A soft glistening rain coated his body.

The boys screamed! Their bodies were racked with pain, then spiraled into ecstasy before fading into numbness. When the mist subsided Roth collapsed on the forest floor. His eyes slowly opened. There was Saba, his back torn to shreds by the protruding wings of a warrior. Staen was curled up in a ball; his fingers long and pointy, skin etched with the elegant, esoteric design of the mark of a monk.

***

And then Roth saw his father's boot. He followed up the length of the man's torso until he met his father's eyes. A solitary tear had escaped and rolled down the man's cheek.

"Come, my son," his father managed to speak through the shivering crack of lips on his worn face. Roth reached to grab his father's leathery hand. "With me. To the mines."

But behind his father's shoulder was a slowly burning light, a star expanding. As it grew larger, winds ripped through the village. Naked young men, now christened warriors, miners, and monks, scattered as rain poured violently into the atmosphere. Trees bent, houses lost their thatched roofs, monks clutched their precious parchments running for safety, crying to the heavens, their sacred ritual desecrated by some unforeseen force.

Emerging with a sonic boom from the light, a large vessel appeared. It was made of a strange, living, ever-changing platinum. It moved through space like liquid. It seemed like hours, but only minutes had elapsed as it hovered over Roth and his father, trapping them in its path.

A hatch opened. Out strode a man in a tight, blue and black suit that seemed to swim over his body. The skin that rippled over his muscular frame was a ripe purple. His hair was a long, flowing mane of star-burst strands, glowing with a fire the people of Roa had never seen. He spoke.

"Roth F'_iiosf of Roa!"

Roth's father held the boy tightly, his tears turning to fiery determination. "What do you want with my son?! My family has suffered enough disappointment today!"

"Roth F'_iiosf of Roa! I am the Destroyer. You have walked through that mist! Rise and take your place with the true champions of this universe. The Light has chosen you, so it must be! Roth F'_iiosf of Roa is no more. Now there is only Black Mage of the Galactic Legion!"

Roth pulled away from behind his father. As the wind and light swirled around them, the boy took a step. He looked at his father, at the man's crumpled face, sunken and desperate for breath. The sagging, tar-pitched skin. Roth took another step toward the Destroyer. He remembered tying twine to mup bugs. He said, sadly, to his father, "I don't want to be a miner."

He took yet another step, then more, and followed the Destroyer into the vessel and disappeared into the black, shapeless void of space.

III.

There's a bar where Rob and Jake are sitting. Its rickety bar stools seem to spill out of the large windows of the place and onto the street. They're facing the television and talking over dance beats. It's easy to ignore the monotonous Robin Thicke remixes, Jake thinks suddenly, when your excessively handsome friend Rob is unloading a fresh batch of college football stories in that wide, cavernous voice of his.

"I was the best arm coach had, but he had me playing tight end," Rob explains, thudding his beer on the counter in subtle protest. "Like, yeah, I was the biggest motherfucker with any kind of skill set he ever recruited, but damn, man, I never wanted to play tight end! Got caught on a slant route with no protection—"

"No protection?" Malik suddenly has his caramel arms around Rob's thick, black ex-football neck. "Sounds like my kind of game."

"There you are!" Rob stands up, almost out of some strange courtesy, and lets Malik steal his seat in the suddenly crowding bar. "Where ya'll been?"

Casper is adjusting his belt, fumbling with his wallet. He pushes his glasses back onto his doughy face twice before even reaching the guys at the bar.

"It's not that kind of party," Jake informs Malik. "We were discussing slant routes. Again." Jake is wearing another striped polo shirt, drinking another Manhattan.

"Child, please. I'd rather hear about any kind of route than about some ridiculous star war or green goblet for the thirtieth time," Malik confides.

"Are you two together? Again?" Jake asks, almost scandalously.

Malik looks over at Casper, who is awkwardly shaking Rob's mammoth hand. Casper, pushing up his glasses again, tiny hairs peaking out of his over-worn Green Lantern t-shirt. In Malik's mind they are piling into Casper's Peugeot, then wandering some dingy comic book store, and Casper's talking to the guy at the counter about rare masks. Then they're at Subway, the green and yellow tile work of the restaurant blending with the smell of rancid banana peppers and dim lighting like an unbalanced psychotropic flash until Malik's nauseous and ready to go. But they're also in a tent on a moss-covered rock, and they're in a forest; they're on the beach under a peach-colored sun.

"No," Malik says, a lilt of reflection in his voice. "No, we're not," he reaffirms, stronger this time and with a hint of sass.

"Oh." Jake is a wise and average fool. His shoes are white New Balances, his checkered boardshorts from Marshall's sales rack, but as Malik puts it, when they're all in the hotel room, his near-useless app start-up, money-strengthened bank account is, essentially, black and gold Prada, to say nothing of Dolce and/or Gabbana.

"Don't worry about what shoes I'm wearing," Jake says, taking off his cross trainers. He holds up one of them, models it. Rob lets out a roaring laugh. Malik clamps his nose with his fingers, tries to make for the door. Inevitably, Jake's musty shoe ends up following Malik around the room.

Casper sits nervously at the edge of the bed, fiddling with the remote, muttering under his breath. Nothing is on, yet he stares vacantly at the snowy screen as if he's reading in between the harsh lines of scattered static. He pushes his face toward the screen. Something materializes, he believes. A ghost outline among the fuzz and low noise? He can hear it speaking—"We're under attack—*bbzztt*—we're outnumbered—*bbzztt*—Load the—There's no time! Mayday! Mayday! Universal quadrant 8923—"

"Cas." Rob tries to make contact. "Cas!" Everything in the room stops. They're all looking at Casper. "What are you doing, dude?"

"I'm trying to ... it's the television." Casper explains, "It's the television. Apparently, you need to be a Shi'ar tech sergeant of the Imperial Court if you're going to figure out how to work this thing."

They all share puzzled looks. Malik shrugs at them, equally clueless. Rob turns back to Casper.

"We didn't come out this way to look at TV, man." Rob walks over to his fidgety friend, puts his hand on Casper's shoulder, then works the thick, mealy flesh of it underneath the shirt. "Let's get loose."

Casper runs out of the room, nearly knocking Jake into a nightstand. Casper beats on the elevator buttons. They all light up, but the elevator doesn't come in time. He sinks to the floor and covers his face with his hands. Malik gingerly walks over to him, stands there, mustering great patience. Casper looks up through a thin veil of tears. Malik is holding his hand out toward him.

"Come on," Malik says, softly, sternly. "Let's go back."

IV.

A small, blue light flashed on.

A man with metallic skin stood in the middle of a vast control room.

"Ion-1." And the rest of the lights sparked to life with a trail of whirring electronics sweeping over the room. "Commence cryobirth. Stage 2."

An array of sleep chambers, nineteen of them. Each one slowly opened in a frozen cloud. Beings emerged from slumber, some gasping, tasting the sterile air of the cryo-chamber, others feeling no real effect at all.

The Destroyer was one of them, his hair cascading away from him as he flexed his awakening muscles.

"Fucking balls, mate," said Spike. He was a tiny man with raw, unkempt hair, still covered in dirt. "What a trip, eh?"

The being next to him, roguish, nearly eight feet tall with green, cratered skin, groaned and pulled himself out of the sleep casket.

"Aw, dreaming about those Crabgirls in the Nebulaar Sector again, Grok?" Spike quipped.

"*@***@*@****@@@*," the large, green man countered.

"Crikey, Ion-1, we're asleep in these stupid metal trash cans for god knows how long, and you can't find time to fix the bloody translators? I don't know how you were picked to be a part of this ragtag outfit if you can't do your one bloody, fucking job, you pooz!"

"Ion-1 was chosen the same way we all were, Spike." Void was standing in front of her, still groggy, still submerged comrade. As she speaks, her skin glosses over in the coat of living pixels that make up her outer nervous system.

"He was chosen by the Light," a voice interrupted. That seemed to shut up the diminutive Spike. A man emerged from his pod, a cloud of smoke alight with blood red embers surrounding him, his chest beating a miniature quasar.

"Red Star. Sir. You have awakened."

"Indeed I have, Ion-1." Red Star stood there naked, pulsating. "Let us forget the translators for now. We have a more pressing matter. Before we left the last quadrant, I felt a surge in energy. Can you play back all significant electro-scans in the last three sleep cycles?"

"Christ, can we all get some clothes on before you start in with all the *Star Trek* shit, mate? I'm freezing me bloody arse off here!"

The Destroyer looked at him, first quizzically, then nodded. "Fine. All members of the Galactic Legion, convene in the chamber of darkness. Now."

***

A droid, bent and distended, its sockets and circuitry exposed, lifted off the gymnasium floor. It rose with a quirky unease, bracing itself on the wall behind it. A shaft of solid light appeared from its hand. It roared to life, moving impossibly fast. Its saber of light ripped through the atmosphere. It was sent hurtling back, smashing into pieces. Roth landed two feet in front of it, cupped his fist into his open palm, and bowed.

The gym door slid open, startling him. A woman covered in ever-changing pixels glided in.

"Roth." She surveyed the heaps of metal and scrap that decorated the gym floor. "You've been in here since we awoke from cryosleep. Why? What purpose does it serve, thrashing battle-bots in such a way?"

Roth, nearly breathless, closed his eyes, letting the calming hand of his father wash over him. He was chasing mup bugs. He turned to look at Void. "You wouldn't understand."

"There is nothing in the cosmos beyond my understanding, young one. Indeed, my systems have communicated with the very Light that has chosen us as Legion. To have even an audience with the Light is to know vast, infinite knowledge." She looked intently at Roth, her eyes tracing his body as if he were merely a blueprint of himself. "Yet ..." She spoke softer. "Yet I feel that you are an enigma that can't be solved with any postulate known to even my eternal databanks."

"I don't know. I guess I can't just ..." He moved closer to Void. He reached out his hand to touch her face. She didn't flinch or twitch or make any movement to show that Roth had breached her personal space. So he touched her again.

"What is this ritual, human?"

"How alone are you?" he asked. He could feel a slight burn as Void's skin emitted a stinging warmth as it brushed his own flesh.

A red light flashed. The chimes of an alarm fell about them.

"Come, it is time." Void glided across the gym floor. When she looked back at him, her eyes, breaking through their usual medicinal stare, seemed to glance back at him sweetly—though Roth could have imagined it, projecting the light of human feeling onto someone, something that he probably shouldn't.

***

A large star map floated above the table. All nineteen members of the Galactic Legion were assembled. They sat in front of crude runes depicting each of their talents. Glassbird sat before crystal wings. Phaser sat before a swirling black hole. The Destroyer's hardened, menacing visage slightly cracked when Roth entered the chamber. He was often proud of his protégé, the one he found on that tiny speck of a planet, Roa, after wading through countless files, sitting in concert with countless sorceresses.

He felt destined to find a Legionaire whose valor would crack the cosmos into shards only to reshape it with ash, goodness, and power. So many times he returned with haggard souls with minimal powers and stout hearts. So many times their bodies would reject the Light, or the Light would reject them, hurling them from the ship into space. The cosmos was littered with the husks of the Destroyer's failures.

When he returned with Roth, Void plugged him into the heart of their ship, feeding him fuel and nourishments to last years in deep space. Roth's body hadn't rejected the Light, hadn't convulsed from diatonic overload. The Destroyer could finally smile.

Red Star sat at the head of the long table in front of a swirling, pulsing image of a red sun. His eyes danced with flame. Roth had very few encounters with him, though he never tired of the Destroyer's many tales of Red Star's valor.

"My friends, my greatest comrades," Red Star began.

"Here we go," Spike mumbled, nudging Roth in the kidney.

"I've troubling news. It seems as if the Vanq have found their way to this sector." A murmur trickled through the assembly. "I know, the Vanq even gives me pause. They are led by the treacherous lech of a lord, Apox, the demon who found the accursed Dark Rose and smashed through many hells to be birthed into this universe.

"His is a vast, insidious evil. At his employ are some of the sickest mercenaries from the darkest galaxies. The Iduwanda pirates of Xon. Cyx the Unicorn Killer and his tribe of cannibal mercenaries. Dragon Deth, the beast wranglers from V-21."

"Yeah, yeah, yeah, we know all about these tossers," Spike spat out, leaning back in his chair, his boots planted on the table. "But what makes this so special, eh? Why the bloody Christ are we worried about these arseholes now? We put them in stasis before, we'll put them in stasis again."

"I'll field this one, sir." Ion-1 stood, proceeded to the center of the table, typing furiously on a touchscreen. "If we're mapping the power surge that Red Star, our incorrigible leader, felt right before the last sleep cycle, and if we're to believe that these are Apox and his forces using power heretofore unknown to them to traverse the stars, we can find out exactly where they are going."

With the touch of another button, the star map whirled and disappeared. Animated pixels rose in its place and coalesced into the shape of a small sphere. It was a small, blue planet with nebulous clouds circling its stratosphere.

"They're headed for Earth," Spike whispered.

"Not that shithole," Grok protested through his gravelly voice, his translator coming online in time for his slanderous quip.

Something about the blue sphere hypnotized Roth. He stared intently. It was not unlike Roa. The stories Spike told of it were entertaining, but mostly seemed to make the young man sad. He asked, "What makes Earth so special?"

"Not earth not earth not earth not earth not earth not earth." Spike was shaking his head, his eyes protruding dangerously out of their sockets.

"Earth is the nexus of the universe," Void offered. "The prophecy of the Light. It ends on Earth." A silence etched over the room. "It all ends on Earth."

Red Star lowered his eyes. His hair turned to fire. He stood up, mouth agape.

A large explosion blew a hole in the roof. The Galactic Legion looked up in unison. Through the breach they could see out into space! The explosion had ripped through the hull, tore down the hallways of the ship, and penetrated the chamber of darkness. A swarm of armor-clad mercenaries with advanced weaponry spilled into the room. Their faces and exposed flesh were covered in a strange slime. The ship itself screamed, jerked its liquid platinum shell as it seemed to writhe in pain.

Glassbird flew into action, her mighty wings ripping through her enemies, striking down three of them. A large hand grabbed her face and flung her into the chamber walls with all its might.

It belonged to a snarling beast of a man made of black soot. Steam and smoke rose from his eyes. Lava filled his mouth.

Two bee-like creatures stepped out from behind him, raised the long prods they held in their hands, and fired them at the still-dazed Glassbird, sending an intense shock through her crystalline body. Electricity spiraled through Glassbird in a near atomic flash, shattering her.

"No!" Spike yelled.

The horde descended on the Galactic Legion. Spike jumped onto the table, confused about where to strike. Two waves of electricity escaped from the bee creatures' rods. One hit Grok, who was being held down by mercenaries. Another hit Red Star, who had managed to tangle up a few mercs in his powerful, heat-charged hair. He exploded, steam rising off of him. His costume was tattered, but he remained practically unharmed, as the lifeless bodies of the mercenaries dropped to the floor.

Grok was not so fortunate. His hollowed-out husk turned to ash before their eyes. Spike leaped from the table. Two large, bony pegs grew out of his palms. He yelled in pain as he bounced off a mercenary's back and sent him hurtling straight for the large man made of black soot.

"AAAPOOOXXX! DIE, YOU BLOODY POOF!" he screamed, and wedged the pegs in his eyes.

Apox stammered. His men were being cut down now that the Legion had regathered and regrouped. For all his vast cosmic power, to be felled by a scruffy turd of a man from Earth? With a wave of his hand, he smacked Spike off of him, sending him hurtling through the air.

"Cripes, this is gonna hurt," Spike whimpered. But before he hit the wall, his spine already irreparably damaged by Apox's blow, Void appeared in mid-air, teleporting him away.

"We've got to get that bastard out of here!" Spike yelled. "I put two charges on those spikes, no telling what kinda damage it'll do mixed up with all of that demon power!"

"Your request is inarticulate," Void said, laying her friend down a few feet from the battle. "But I know what must be done."

She teleported away.

Apox, with Spike's pegs still submerged into his eyes, stood over Roth. He smelled of acid, shit, and brimstone. Roth's fists were bloody and caked with the pulp of dead space pirates.

Facing death, Roth's time with the Galactic Legion flooded his memory. He could feel the crack of a bamboo pole crash down on his back, the war-hungry laughter of the Destroyer imploring him to rise every time, to walk through mountains and jungles on unexplored planets to fight strange, ravenous beasts with nothing but a stick and stone. They had saved so many villages on so many backwater planetoids against Red Star's commands, several times turning "observe and report" missions into liberating sprees. However, Roth eventually grew weary of the Destroyer's cruel, guiding hand. One night, the two covered in blood, doused in a heavy rain in a briar-thick jungle, Roth threw down his fighting staff. "Here," he told him. "I don't want to kill anymore."

The Destroyer laughed. Roth continued, "For two years we've ravaged and revenged throughout the galaxy, yet murder and slavery and subjugation still persist. I'm done with it."

The Destroyer took Roth's head into his hands and kissed him deeply. His mouth was so warm on Roth's lips, his tongue so thick, so slicked with saliva. When the Destroyer pulled away he bellowed another laugh. "My boy! It was always your decision to stay and fight or to run and hide! Though we are bound by a code of freedom, of liberation, we are not obliged to follow if our heart does not insist!"

Roth nearly turned away, somewhat angry over the kiss, but angrier still. "No! There is not only running and hiding. There is not only making war, or writing holy texts, or mining for ore. There is ... there's something else." He looked into his former teacher's eyes that day in the rain, a cackle of lightning illuminating the sky. "I intend to find it, this other thing. I intend to stay."

They returned to the ship in silence, furtive glances only strengthening that silence in the months that followed. Soon the Destroyer would find another protégé while uncovering another sorceress in another universe with another prophecy for him to solve, to find another player in Red Star's game. As much as he liked to destroy, he would often defy his namesake; the Destroyer could, in his own way, somehow build. Roth would be left to meditate alone in his room, searching. Left to thinking endlessly about his father, about Saba, about Roa.

And now Apox.

The large creature leaped into the air. Roth jumped. He didn't know what to do. Aim for the eyes? Try to drive Spike's spikes farther into Apox's head? He had an eighth of a second to do it.

As the two met in the chamber of Darkness, a light flashed. Roth rolled right through it and crashed into the meeting table. Red Star emerged. They could see a similar light appear in space. Void was outside, holding Apox in her arms, floating away from their ship. A voice sounded in Roth's head. "We are never alone." It echoed, sounding like Void's.

Then, in the black of space, among debris and craggy asteroids, an explosion trailed like a falling star.

V.

"What do you mean, they're coming?" Jake snickers from the backseat of Casper's Peugeot, biting his quivering lower lip. "Who's coming?" He can barely whisper the words without painfully fighting back a laugh.

Casper looks in the rear-view mirror, adjusts it, eyeing Jake. His stuffy green and white polo shirt, strangely stiff blond hair, dangerously jaundiced skin, over-dyed Old Navy jean shorts and dreadful, ever-present white tennis shoes—"I've got bad feet," Chris had said the other night when Malik was making fun of his "boring guy" uniform at Olive Garden. "You've got bad everything, hon," Malik reminded him, tossing a grape tomato at Jake, laughing. Always laughing.

Casper stares out into the parking lot. A bird shitting on the curb impresses a bum so much, he stands up, pointing and guffawing, knocking paper bags full of glass bottles into the gutter.

Static hangs in the air. Casper can feel it through his fingers. Right? Can't he feel it? Sitting there in the 7-Eleven parking lot, he grips the steering wheel, watches a newspaper swiftly levitate into the air and swirl around the dancing bum. Casper shuts his eyes and tightens his grip. "Come on, come on," he whispers. There's a sucked-out silence, a nothingness.

When the door opens it's like a wall of sound crumbling into the front seat. Malik and Rob are on the tail end of a bad joke. "I told him I'm not paying for it. Those items were flawed."

"But, Malik, you put them on, wore them outside, and everything? They can't resell underwear after they've been all over your man areas," Rob informs him through a light chuckle.

They fall into their respective seats, Malik settling into the front, gleefully sipping a Slurpee, willfully oblivious to any emotion Casper could be conjuring; Rob in back, careful not to let his leg slide too far over to Jake's side before he could spiral into a sad trance of guilt and the dark dread that arises when he's near Jake, mesmerized by that strange doe-eyed look as Jake's lumpy body lay there after they had fucked that night a few years ago.

Rob looks over at Jake's face now and sees another kind of confusion. He mouths, "What's going on now?"

Jake, wide-eyed, just shakes his head. The only thing the two of them had in common was their infatuation with the strangeness of Malik and Casper, two gentlemen with even less in common but even more emotionally entwined than Rob and Jake ever were.

Rob stares forward and thinks about a life with Jake where they're walking dogs or shopping for flourescent light bulbs at Target, or suffering through a three hour-long Gay Men's Choir Christmas special. He shudders and turns to see Jake picking his own nose. Any guilt he feels slowly melts and re-coagulates into self-pity.

The best arm on the team in a Peugeot at a 7-Eleven in Myrtle Beach with three other fags. Yet, despite his continued reservations about the inanities of mundane gay life, he is slowly growing comfortable. So when he looks at Jake, Malik, and Casper, Rob just shakes his head and cracks a wry smile, letting the Barbara Tucker and Ultra Naté beat his eardrums with their sweet romance.

He asks, "Casper, you all right?"

They're already on the road. There's a hushed, blossoming twilight peaking over the horizon.

Is the air thick with electricity?

Malik shifts in his seat. He finally looks over to Casper, wordlessly pleads for the pudgy man to say,

"Yes, yes, I'm fine."

"And this is my Green Lantern collection." They were in his room in his tiny apartment in University City. "You've got John Stewart," Casper said, picking up a small, green-clad figurine. "And this is Guy Gardener. This is Kilowog." Before him on a tiny IKEA dresser stretched various miniatures of the entire Green Lantern Corps. And posters of star-crossed barbarians in dragon-skin loin cloths, of men in long, flowing capes and armed to the teeth with an irrational amount of guns.

"What?" Casper looked from the dresser toward Malik, his face flush.

"No, nothing." Malik looked for a place to sit and found a corner of the bed that wasn't smothered in paraphernalia. "It's just not what I'm used to."

"Oh," Casper said, his once assured voice turning more delicate as the conversation started to turn. "What exactly are you used to?"

"I don't know," Malik replied. He cleared another section of the bed. Casper almost gasped as a pile of comics tumbled onto the floor. "Here." Malik patted the empty space. "Sit."

Casper sat. Surprising himself, he leaned into Malik and rested his head on his shoulder. "You didn't have to do that. Earlier."

"What do you mean?" Malik asked, his eyes trailing over Casper's soft form.

"You didn't have to say what you said to those guys. You didn't have to stand up to them like that. Thank you."

"Oh." Malik let out a sigh. "That. Well, honestly they were out of line. It just felt—I don't know, whatever, it felt wrong."

"Social capital is not easy to give up."

"Besides, my motives were not totally pure," Malik growled into Casper's ear. "You're cute."

"Oh, yeah?" Casper took off his oversized Captain America t-shirt. His pale, floppy white skin and hairy chest dangled off his curvy body. "Prove it."

A year later they are going 85, then 95 miles an hour on the turnpike, flying recklessly around small suburban towns and making wild turns onto one-way streets.

"Oh Lord Jesus, Judy, and Liza!"

Jake is a mess of nerves in the backseat. Rob is panicking and yelling for Casper to calm down. Malik has his eyes closed, and he's muttering for god and Jesus and Buddha under his breath. Casper drives.

"Do something, motherfucker!" Jake screams at Rob. His face has twisted into a maze of frowning skin. "You're always on about your great physical prowess, about how fucking brilliant you were on the goddamn field! When it comes right down to it, you're a scared little faggot, just like the rest of us. Aren't you? Aren't you?!?!"

Rob sits in stunned silence as buildings whiz by, as stoplights beg for the Peugeot to stop. The road beneath them shrinks as their vehicle plunges into the night. One hundred miles per hour, but nothing is happening for Rob except Jake's rant in slow motion. His distorted, admonishing contortions. For this moment in time, Rob finally sees the man—Jake, in all of his start-up, coding, Old Navy wearing glory—as a man.

What is this person like? Is Jake just a shopping trip to Walgreens every Tuesday? A man DVRing Dr. Oz and Young and the Restless? Is Jake just a man sitting at a bar, laughing at bad jokes and hoping for a Lady Gaga song to come spiraling out of the jukebox?

Rob doesn't know. He reaches out and slaps Jake in the face.

Malik unbuckles his seatbelt. He turns to Casper and wrenches the man's grip from the steering wheel. Casper is blank, time-suspended and zombie-like, but his grip is tight. He is muttering, "Not the earth not the earth not the earth not the earth," when a flashing white light appears down the road.

"Casper! Let go of the fucking wheel!" Malik screams.

The light gets larger, brighter, whiter, wider, until it is no longer simply a light. It is a fissure, a chasm opening, roaring thunder. A slick, silver orb peaks through the breach. "Oh, my god," Rob whispers, his hand landing on Jake's bare knee.

The car swerves into a guard rail, flips over a ditch, and rams upside down into a light pole. The wheels don't even spin.

Malik's eyes clog with a broken murkiness. He can smell the acidic aroma of iron and blood. *Lights are flashing?* Everything is black and white and upside down. He can see two figures walk toward him. Their boots are heavy. Their walk is locked in and measured. They're speaking in tongues so strange they sound metallic. The lights turn into a single, burning sphere. It's a white vortex cutting through the black night. Wind whips, and everything around him trickles away like bits of a sand castle floating off into an embroiled sea.

He can't fully make them out, but the three figures are standing above him: one a purplish black shadow with laughing gray teeth; another with windswept hair that seems sentient, alive, on fire; and the last, a wire of a man, boyish and tar black, his cloak flitting in the wind like wings as he pulls himself closer to the car with his long staff.

The car tears away around them. The metal, leather, plastic, and iron tear away into the night. Flaccid bodies ooze across the ditch. Malik watches Jake and Rob slide away from the debris. Casper floats, unconscious, into the air, still attached to his car seat, limply banging against the seat belt and leaking blood onto Malik's face.

Malik pulls himself up. Pain shoots through his body. He lets out a bestial scream. Panting, he looks toward the three figures. The one with the staff has his hand raised in his direction. He can see blood bubbling up under the being's nose, his eyes strain, and a thick vein throbs at his temple. Casper lowers to the ground behind him.

"What do you want with him?!"

The man with the stringy hair and graying skin speaks.

"Malik El Amin of the planet Vronson-vi-7, the one true Earth! How do you question our presence? Have you not heard our message? Have you not heard it screaming through the void? I am the Destroyer. Step now into the Light."

From his knees and wracked with pain, Malik looks at Casper face-down in the ditch, his lips drinking mud. *What a strange boy.*

Slowly, Casper's eyes crack open. He stares right into the searing light surrounding the three mysterious figures silhouetted in the balmy atmosphere. Malik is but a shadow juxtaposed against them, but somehow it fits. Casper smiles, then closes his eyes again.

"They're here," Malik whispers in between frantic sobs. "They've finally come."

Optimum Body

Pulp was everywhere. In their veins, running through the atmosphere. Thick clouds of it burst through cracks in the windows and settled into their skin.

Everyone everywhere was dying. Lying across overturned garbage cans, straddling grates, steam billowing up over bodies, community centers, and hovels, exasperated.

There were no park benches anymore. The few that still existed were argued over by the strung out and desperate, who staked their claim by pissing on them. Pulp meant you had it bad, not like anything you've ever had laced with anything else you ever had. It was its own raw, unfiltered thing. Pulp was something unusual.

The few who made their way through the city streets walked with a purpose. They went to their jobs, performed whatever tasks—bashing keys, laying bricks, stuffing microchips into husks and compartments, monitoring shit, calculating or diagramming whatever a decent bot couldn't— minutia, really, troubleshooting, that kind of work.

The trains were a mess, but they ran. Twenty years into pulp's rise, though, and you'd still see an old lady or two on a robo-bus, crouching in a seat, twiddling knitting needles, or more likely, staring into the void.

Glaq took public transit, even though he didn't have to. He read a newspaper. He would sit in a cafe and stare out of the window. The harsh light was oceanic in its reach. Everything in these places was illuminated. Outside was darkness. Outside were pulpheads turned into ogres, walking in deadened trances and falling into abandoned cars head first. Their eyes popped out of their skulls like feral cartoons. He still carried a watch.

"Thanks." He paid the tattooed man behind the counter, glancing at his wrist. He folded the paper under one arm and put the other one through the sleeve of his coat. A mistake, but the man could see Glaq's gun as it peeked out of a not-so-secret compartment in the coat's lining.

"Nice piece," the man said.

Glaq narrowed his gaze at him. He noticed the other tattoo—not the one of a fish-like outline in bad black ink that the man had tried to conceal under his collar. No use in alerting the diner's owners that he was a Dolphin, one of the worst street gangs, in his past life. That was of no concern. It was the number 13, the two asterisks, and the letter A that alarmed Glaq. The man behind the counter had gone to BioGen and had selected a body.

"I'm slipping," Glaq said under his breath. He shook his head and turned to leave.

"Is that yours?" the man called after him.

"Yeah. I'm a Palladin. Whatever that even means anymore."

"Nah," he replied. "Nah, I've seen Palladins." The man cocked an angular smile. A sudden intensity burned across his face. His off-white complexion showed weird splotches. "Ha, I've definitely seen some Palladins." His grin was now evil. Glaq cringed at the thought that this man might have killed one of his brothers. "Anyway, nah, is that your body? Or did you choose, too?"

Glaq cinched his coat and tilted his head, half-nod/half-shake, full scowl. He could feel his fists tighten in the coat pockets. Not wanting to engage, he stepped outside. He looked back at the sneering cook behind the counter. Patrons had started filling the cafe, brushing past him. He could feel his piece jostling around inside his coat, somehow sprung loose from its compartment as if making an attempt to jump into his hand, begging to spend its charged shells.

**

"We had to be so young when pulp first hit the streets," Zev announced. He opened a cellophane packet, cursing himself as he dropped the piping hot thing on the desk. Glaq stood in the doorway and watched the man stuff his face with prefab. "What, seven, eight years old?"

The computer screen in front of them popped on. Its blue screen illuminated both of their faces. Zev patted the empty chair beside him with his fat hands. Glaq still stood, watching the screen dance to life. It was something else he enjoyed watching, these old screens crack on, as if they were dialing themselves in from another time.

Zev barely had the patience for these things anymore, and it was showing. After every third or fourth keystroke, his eyes darted around the keyboard, looked beyond the monitor for something, or he'd let out a huff and stare blankly at the screen.

"I'm not sure what you're looking for here, Glaq. There's not much in these old thumb drives that you can't find at the MindCenter. I mean, every pulphead kid has a BioLens nowadays, could tell you exactly what you're looking for."

Glaq shifted, let slip a sigh. "Did you find the file?"

Zev put down his prefab. His chubby face tightened. He ran his fingers through his bright, floral-patterned blue hair. Though the room was dark, the screen's light sparkled from the piping running through Zev's clothing, which seemed to segment the man's big body. "Will you sit?" Zev asked. The heft had left his voice. There was only a curious, pleading inquiry. Glaq took a step inside, his eyes locked on Zev.

"Is that it?" Glaq said, pointing. Zev's eyes followed his finger. There was a white box floating on the screen, suspended there as if in amber.

Zev's sigh was filled with sullen anger. Glaq shifted uncomfortably, but still crossed his arms and leaned against the opposite wall. "Yep. That's it. The Commander's BioGen file. Honestly, I don't know what could be in here that's not in the public record."

"Let me be the one to figure that out," Glaq said with an accidental vitriol. "Just ... print it out."

"Print it out?" Zev laughed, his ample belly bouncing in the glow of the screen.

"Yes, print it out, download it, send it to me, whatever. Just get me the file. Christ."

Zev cleared his throat and started typing. Glaq stared and watched the man. Zev's hands danced around the keys wildly, a certain jazz to his pecking and plinking. His memory was fully charged, delighting in the joy of touching hardware, listening to the hum of a modem. Glaq found himself shaking his head. He could swear that there were sparks coming from Zev's soft fingers.

"OK, as you might have guessed, a lot of this stuff is encrypted and pretty much all of it on this thumb drive is incompatible with anything we have at MindCenter or any common unit," Zev remarked, not even looking up from the keyboard. "But if you give me a few minutes, I can get this cracked for you and sent over to someone in the lab to reformat."

A pause, then Glaq placed his hand on Zev's shoulder. Another pause. Zev closed his eyes and put his hand on Glaq's, kneading the familiar, calloused skin.

"I'm—Glaq, I'm getting it." Zev said quietly.

"I know," Glaq responded, his voice a soothing timbre, like a grandmother's at Easter dinner.

"I'm getting a body. Bio's paying for it, you know, after the merger with MindCenter. We're all getting new bodies, Glaq. It's—it's going to be—"

Glaq closed his eyes, squeezing Zev's hand tight. "I know."

Zev hit Send.

Glaq yanked Zev upwards with one hand and closed the door behind them. Zev weighed 300 lbs but floated into the air like paper. He fell into his arms, his face resting on the other man's chest. Glaq ran his fingers through Zev's stubbly hair, massaging his scalp with gentle circular motions. A tear slowly made its way down Zev's face. Glaq stared at the salty orb as it burst on his cheek. Then, in a huff, he licked it, his tongue lapping over Zev's face. His stubble felt coarse—like a rusted steel mesh of tiny, fibrous wires poking through cables. Glaq gnawed at the man's face until he met his lips, could feel Zev panting, his breath a desperate wind.

"Don't," Zev whispered.

Glaq pushed him away, sliding out of his jacket in the same motion. He reached for the man's waist and pulled his shirt off over his head. Zev's wonderful frame came to life, free of that tight garment. Folds of flesh fell everywhere. Glaq dove into his chest, his tongue working every piece of his torso. Smelling the familiar scent of prefab and cinnamon, his nose nuzzled into the crevice of Zev's sweaty breasts.

Glaq caressed the man's shoulders—rugby-wide,

powerful, and compact—his long fingers working over the blades softened by Zev's back cellulite. Zev tried to straighten up, tried not to melt right there, but the combination of Glaq's sinewy body close to his own, his wet tongue darting over his body, his hands turning his back into mush, he simply let go.

Glaq was half a foot taller, darker skinned—pure onyx black. Zev's skin was an ecru oak. Glaq thought they looked great with their bodies commingled.

When they were both at the academy they'd bunked together. They'd walked through the radiant fields, decoded mines that triggered sarin gas by pheromones, meditated together in deserts and at the bottoms of abandoned mines, snakes and scorpions creeping over their toes in the heat, propped up against cacti.

The Commander suspected they were sharing their bodies at night and would punish them the next day before dawn.

"You'll fight!" he told them.

A circle of stone. Inside, the two young men wearing electro-gloves would battle hand-to-hand with the entire camp watching. They couldn't fake it. Full contact combat until one of them would fall. The Commander made an example out of them. No Palladin would surrender to the temptation of the flesh; no Palladin could be pure of mind if such thoughts burned bright in his.

Glaq's rubbing soon went deeper, turning the tissue under Zev's skin gelatinous. His fervor grew. He groped and grabbed at Zev's ass, shoved his hands down his pants, feeling and fondling, fingers searching out crevices and cracks, running through pubic hair, gripping at genitalia.

Zev started to tighten up. He gently gripped Glaq's wrist. He couldn't stop the man if he wanted to. Glaq's arms went slack. Zev pushed him back an inch, then stepped back another inch himself. Then another. Stepping out of his pants, softly tossing them aside. His thighs were so thick they touched. Flesh welled up at his waist, his cock hung like a fat slab of prefab as it poked out from under his ample belly.

Zev reached behind himself and felt for the desk, then boosted himself up on top of it. He kept his legs closed. Glaq felt his body and mind slowing as he disrobed. His asymmetrical t-shirt with the raw hemline, his patchwork pants, his combat boots. He felt the cool of the floor run up through the soles of his bare feet. This made his dick hard.

He approached Zev slowly, gently, and looked into his welling-up eyes. Glaq stopped when he got close enough to Zev sitting on the desk that he could touch his knee. He rubbed his hand over the knot and slowly made his way down. Getting on his own knees, he popped Zev's moonboots off his feet and watched his stubby toes wiggle. Glaq opened up each one and slid his tongue around one foot, nibbling at the tiny hairs on the knuckles, making sure to take in the smell.

Zev writhed in absolute ecstasy. Slowly, Glaq stood up, making sure not to take his mouth off of Zev's body, making sure not to take his hands off of his thighs. His hands slipped down Zev's inner thigh. He didn't move them any farther until Zev, shivering at his touch, parted them wide and let him slip his naked body in between.

He lunged forward and wildly kissed Zev on his open mouth, their tongues swimming in each other. Each breath was a connected, cosmic movement of their lungs. Zev tried his best to wrap his legs behind Glaq's back until he was able to. His bulbous feet tied like a bow, seeming to sprout like wing's from Glaq's back.

He reached up under Zev's ass and yanked the man forward until his butt hung off the desk by inches.

Zev's head hit the computer monitor with a soft thud. Glaq reached to rub the top of his friend's head, but Zev grabbed his hand and inserted Glaq's fingers into his mouth. Slowly, he slid his head up and down on the digits, first one, then two, three—loud, aggressive slurps leaving a trail of saliva behind.

His fingers slicked, Glaq used them to search Zev's butthole and slowly plunged them inside. Zev moaned deeply, a manly growl, trying desperately to hold onto an air of rigid masculinity. After the third thrust, though, he couldn't. His body fell limp, and his moans became higher pitched.

Glaq stopped probing for awhile. He bent toward Zev, kissed him, and then went lower until his mouth was on Zev's cock. The head was so round, the shaft so fleshy; stubby, tight, slick—not very long, so Glaq could swallow it whole. Zev bucked, then tapped him on the head as if to say "Slow—not yet."

Glaq obliged and pulled his mouth away. He gripped Zev by the ankles, hoisted them up over his shoulders. Zev's head gently thudded against the computer monitor again. Glaq squatted under his rear.

Zev's ass cheeks were spread open like two, glorious hills, his hole a throbbing valley. Taking a breath, Glaq plunged his tongue into Zev's deep hole, lapping and sucking until it was moist, loose. He watched the man's rosebud brighten, using his tongue, mouth, lips to widen it. Glaq stood up, pulling his face from the dewy cavern of Zev's sweet, hot butt, his long cock bouncing in between his legs. He put the tip of his dick at Zev's hole.

Zev was squirming, yanking his legs open wider, nodding his head, biting his lip. His eyes shot open. The head of Glaq's dick was inside of him. A shimmer poured over Zev's body, a solar flare erupting in deep space set to singe the planets in its wake. Another half inch, then another. Zev clenched, pushed Glaq out, and closed his asshole. Glaq tilted his head, tried to read the man. Zev sucked in air and let it go, then opened his hole again, pulled his own legs out even farther, and closed his eyes. Glaq entered fully, and this time Zev smiled.

Glaq was fucking him again, wildly. Totally lost in his thrusts from the moment of entry. He could barely look at his partner, tried not to hear any of the sounds, tried not to smell any of the smells. If he did, if he saw that cherubic face, heard Zev's moans and gasps, the slap of his hard flesh against his, he knew he would cum. He wanted this to last. It would be the last time they'd be truly together.

Holding Glaq's feet in the air, he felt the man's toes wiggle, then stiffen. He looked down, and Zev was cumming, plumes of silky jizz arcing out of his cock. His face contorted, twisting from a shy smile to a grimace, to ecstasy with every volley of hot white liquid squirting out of his cock.

Zev's body slammed into Glaq's midsection as he came, lifting off the table, light as dust, only to slam back down on the hard desk surface. Zev clenched his cheeks as he tensed up, coming so hard it splashed Glaq's face, then releasing. He slid off the table, Glaq's dick sliding out of him with a wet, audible pop, onto his knees. Zev pulled Glaq's penis into his own mouth and sucked on it, deep and hard, gagging on the length.

One final thrust. Zev's throat was now used to it touching his tonsils, used to the taste. Glaq firmly grabbed the back of his head and bobbed the man up and down on his shaft, slowly at first then firmly.

It was strange watching Zev, his eyes open and concentrating on sucking, squirming under him like a pool of jelly and bones—stringy, sticky cum pooling between them, shining in the glow of the computer monitor like a spider's web after a rain. But there was something about the desperation in Zev's post-ejaculate visage that turned him on. Glaq closed his eyes and thrust harder, letting the warmth of his mouth, the muffled whimpers and slight gagging sounds unravel in his mind a wild and fantastic feeling, those glorious sounds, until he found himself cumming in big, bulbous bursts.

He let go of Zev's head before he came. That seemed to confuse Zev a bit. The man slurped vigorously until he felt the thick cream coat the roof of his mouth. He swallowed the first blast hungrily, then pulled it out to watch three more thick spurts erupt onto his chest.

Glaq's body shuddered. It felt like the room quaked. A spell of dizziness overcame him. He backed up to the wall and slid down its chalky surface. Zev crawled over to him, put his hand on his chest, and buried his face in Glaq's shoulder.

Glaq stared into the remaining abyss of the room. The blue glow of the computer flashed. "Download complete," it said.

The file was ready. It was time to go. Glaq pressed a finger into Zev's chest and swirled his drying cum around the velvety hairs on Zev's nipples. He watched as his index finger made a whirlpool out of the semen, mesmerized by the concentric movement, trying to both remember Zev's current body, to implant the warmth of it, the inherent heroism in it, into his mind, as well as to forget it completely, to be satisfied with their final act of passion, to remove himself.

***

Glaq played with the lens in his pocket. There was no other way to get the information he needed. He didn't have a computer back at his cell of an apartment, at least nothing compatible with the hardware he'd had Zev dig up. So he borrowed a lens. He popped it in before the robo-bus arrived. The metal hunk of junk slid to a stop on its electric skates. Glaq was surprised to see a human form in the driver's seat. He fished out a credit from his pocket and slammed it into the receptacle, walking up the aisle before he could even figure out if the driver was a real man or not.

He settled into his seat, rubbing his irritated eyes. The lens was not agreeing with him. Everyone that trailed by on the sidewalk, almost all of them mumbling to themselves—out into the ether, into their devices, a chatter of gnashing teeth, clicking lips, and slick tongues—were all several years into the technology. He sat there, trying to figure out how to turn it on.

"Hello?"

He spoke into the air. Digitized, scrolling images of a menu screen appeared before him. Glaq blinked, and the screen went black.

"Loading apps."

An avatar of the earth appeared; so did one file. He imagined some teenaged pulphead would have about fifty such clickable avatars and apps flooding their vision at all times. That was why they were always walking into the street, getting hit by robo-taxis. That, and the fact that pulp nearly zombiefied anyone who took the damn stuff.

The old woman who sat across from him turned to watch him. She adjusted her surgeon's mask and shook her head. The two sat in silence for a block until an alert jarred Glaq from his reverie. The woman beeped twice. She looked at her arm; it glowed. He strained to get a better look, edging up in his seat. On her arm, "13," two asterisks, and the letter C shone like neon lamps.

"It came," she said, in a nearly silent rasp. "It came."

She slowly started to twist, her skin color shifting in the light, turning from a wrinkled and spotty caramel yellow into a smooth, pale slate. No matter how many times Glaq had seen it, it still felt strange to him, seeing a body turn in public. Her eyes flattened, her nose shrank, the stalk of her limbs straightened. It wasn't a full transmission, but he could see her slowly evolve, move toward a pre-selected ideal of perfection.

He noticed her watching him watch her.

"I look fabulous," she declared through her mask. "I look—I look great."

Glaq put his head down into his newspaper. An ad for BioGen caught his eye. Seberis Smythe himself stared back at him, his eyes casting a gaze that seemed to burrow into him. Glaq folded the paper under his arm again and slumped into his seat, fuming.

***

The cook was out back. He'd insisted on walking to the trash cans behind the restaurant despite the alleyway being a spot known for pulpheads. Such alleys often had piles of living human bodies stacked on top of each other, half naked, writhing in the sun. But he needed to feel the release of an actual cigarette and didn't want to hear any shit from the manager. So the cook took a walk.

There was a slight breeze. He sucked it in as he inhaled toxic smoke. He turned to go back, but a hand shoved the cigarette back into his mouth. His throat burned, the taste of raw carcinogenic ash on his tongue. The guy pushed him up against the trash cans with a thud. A body in there moved, groaned.

"You?" he managed to choke out.

"Talk when I tell you to talk," Glaq told him. He pushed up on the cook, inches from his face. "You know what I am. You know what I can do."

"Ha, yeah," the cook laughed in between coughs.

"Fucking Christ. Yeah, I know what you are. I know you fucking got no jurisdiction since BioGen took over for—" Glaq punched the cook in the gut. A plume of smoke erupted from the man's mouth. "Ah ... fuck. What is this, man? Huh?"

"Where did you go for your body?"

"What? I went to BioGen. I stood in line like everyone else. Pristine, nubile, beautiful, white body."

The cook looked Glaq up and down. There wasn't anything particularly beautiful about him. This cook, this former Dolphin, however, was kind of sexy in a "former gangbanger who sold kids a drug that almost wiped out half the Atlantic" kinda way. So his stares made Glaq feel small.

Glaq straightened, narrowed his brow, and instinctively reached for the guy's throat.

"You know what I am. You know what I can do. I think you also know I don't give a damn about jurisdiction right now."

He lifted the cook by the throat and slammed him into the trash can on the opposite side of the alley. Even louder moans emanated from that one.

"Where. Did. You. Go. For your ... body!"

He was in the cook's face. Tears streamed out of a crack in the lens Zev gave him, his eye red and pulsing with blood. Glaq trembled, his forehead on the cook's forehead. The man's eyes darted around; all coolness left him. There was a tremor in his voice as he watched the broken Palladin try to compose himself.

***

The night air cooled. Glaq lifted his jacket around himself, bunched up as tight as he could, neglecting to button the thing. He didn't want to feel constricted.

It was late. He pushed past pulpheads everywhere

and walked up a side street, a warehouse sitting ominously at the road's end. He tried to remain outside of the street lights and stick to the shadows.

Among the steadily moving people—freaks, pulpheads, ultra rich teenagers on benders looking to score—were a group of extremely well-sculpted, blonde-white men, all about the same build, height, and disposition. Their wildly varying attire further summed it up: well-trained, heavily-armed guards.

Glaq moved in, snaking his way around the building, making sure to stay clear of the muscle. He marked one of them and followed him inside, a clean-cut, young-looking man with a careless walk. Even the most well-trained mercenary fell prey to the high of a new body. They made one cocky. There was a certain strut, an unearned assurance. They lost their vigilance.

Glaq slipped out of the shadow and smoothly placed a sleeper hold on the new-body muscle. Once he was out, he plucked out the dude's lens and popped it into his own eye. Everyone kept everything on their fucking lenses these days. The entire schematic of the place laid out before him on a half-inch piece of prismatic glass.

It was a clean walk through the warehouse into a wide loft. The air was thick with smoke. It wasn't from pulp, though. It felt to Glaq like something else.

"It's a neutralizer," a voice called out to him. "It's got twice the potency of pulp, twice the lucid dream-inducing euphoria, and none of the zombie bullshit. Plus ..."

A figure stepped out of a thick patch of fog, wearing a bathrobe of elegant design woven from ultra thin pieces of pure gold.

"... it actually acts as a remedy for pulp infection. One step into this mist and you're cured."

Seberis Smythe emerged with a champagne flute in

his hand.

Glaq reached for his gun.

"I wouldn't," Smythe warned.

Glaq looked around. Bodies moved within the mist. He slowly lowered his hand from his coat.

"Seberis Smythe. You're under arrest for conspiracy to commit genocide."

Smythe laughed flippantly, almost dropping his champagne. "Genocide? Wow, that's a new one." He moved elegantly across the fog-drenched room. "Oh, you think you're the only former Palladin who's come here looking for me? You think you're the only one who has figured it all out?"

A gush of air swooped in, sucking up the dense smoke. Ornate furniture revealed itself in the fog's absence. Men similar to the guards appeared. Most were naked; some in spandex shorts and bare-chested; others were draped on top of each other; all perfectly chiseled and white. Glaq looked into each of their eyes, probing, lens off, searching for the humanity in them.

"Perfection. Absolute perfection." Smythe spun around slowly, taking in all of his creations. "I've changed the world, don't you see, young Palladin—?"

"You've destroyed it. You created pulp to subject half of the population, rob them of their will, so that, when your body project launched, you'd have the other half as a captive audience, willing buyers looking to download their essence into a new shell."

"You make it sound so simple, Palladin. As if there weren't years, decades of planning on my part! I'm actually hurt at how ... Cro-Magnon you make it all seem!"

Smythe moved toward a dresser and sat in front of its mirror, casually tousling his perfect hair, fishing around in a chest of drawers, pulling out a long, white box.

"Look, I'm sorry. No one wants to be weird, or fat, or Black or any of that shit. Everyone wants a fair chance, OK? I'm just—I'm leveling the playing field."

"You're profiting off pain."

"Oh, my god. It is too late in the evening to debate semantics with you."

"And the Palladins."

"What about them?" Smythe perked up. He seemed to slither back toward Glaq, an unease in his eyes. "That band of outmoded ruffians?" Smythe cracked a wry smile as he grandly gestured around the room.

Glaq's shoulders went limp. He stared into their faces again, and he could see them. Le-bo from quadrant 7, who mastered the brier climb in two weeks. Juan from the Derminus Sector, who would sneak hentai and cigarettes into the barracks after curfew. Xian in robotics with the limp, the one who fashioned silicon wings with embedded LED screens out of discarded prefab cellophane.

They all stood around Glaq, their arms crossed or nervously twitching, shifting their stances. He turned to Smythe and finally truly saw him. Smythe pushed the white box toward him and lifted its hinged lid with his forefingers. A long syringe was inside, a glowing neon liquid encased in the glass.

"Join us, my son," Smythe insisted. "Really, you have no choice."

"There's always a choice," Glaq stated, his body straightening. He crouched into a fighting stance, one arm by his face, a foot raised slightly off the ground. "My current body is heroic. So, no thank you ... Commander."

Smythe's face fell, then morphed into a twisted, disgusting sneer that looked nearly inhuman. "Very well, then! I should have had you Palladins destroyed! Kill him!"

The former Palladins moved in on Glaq, guns

drawn, electro-gloves powered up. One lashed out, but he was too slow. Glaq popped his shoulder out of place with one well-placed blow.

Another swung at his abdomen with a powered glove. A swivel, and Glaq avoided the punch—though this guy was clearly faster than the first. Two punches to the face sent the brute reeling.

A half second later, Glaq was punched in the ribs. A quick, hard punch. Glaq tried to push the pain out, tried to meditate. He was back at camp, his back to a cacti, across from him was Zev, smiling through closed eyes, knowing that Glaq was watching him.

"Don't look at me like that," he said through laughter.

"Like what?" Glaq returned.

"Like that," said one of the perfectly chiseled, blonde, former Palladins, a tear welling up in his eyes. With a loud *whoosh*, the fog returned. Thicker, denser, with an aggressive stench.

"What is this?" Smythe—The Commander—demanded.

"This?" the perfect former Palladin asked, still staring at Glaq, waving his hands in the air. "This is pulp." Then he turned to Smythe. "Unfiltered, grade A, factory assembly line-supplied pulp."

All of the former Palladins reached for their throats, covered their mouths and eyes. They scattered into the night, funneling out of the loft down through the warehouse. Some made it to the curb and barfed on the street. The Palladin who remained walked up to Glaq, slipped his gun out of his coat, and pressed his lips up to Glaq's ear.

"Get the fuck out of here," he whispered.

Glaq disappeared into the night. The former Palladin turned to Smythe and pointed the gun at his old Commander's head.

Girls Who Look through Glass

Packs of artisanal biscuits stacked in several rows, shrink wrapped and dusty. Rows of organic pickled sauerkraut in reclaimed mason jars. She wields her box cutter over these items like a samurai with her sword, ripping through splintered cardboard boxes down the aisles decorated with rows of burlap sacks filled with bacon-infused, gluten-free sriracha bars and oat cakes in cellophane bags adorned with pictures of old white men on horses. She slits the top of a package with one precise glide, ignoring the picture of a knife with a *Ghostbusters* slash through it, her blade gently grazing a packet of caramelized seitan chips. She snaps the blade back in its metal sheath and slides it into her back pocket. It's a delicate act of violence.

The aisles are quiet tonight. Minutes ago they were a yammering mix of gentrifiers glued to their cell phones on conference calls and soccer moms shrewish in their investigation of every ingredient in the packs of incense and bags of frozen kale lining their carts. The only time, it seemed to her, that any of them cared about whether something was organic or free-range was if enough of the horde was within earshot. They all seemed to compete for air time: bearded hipsters with their own grocery bags made of hemp rope; hippie nannies in thrifted sundresses still caked in dirt from repairing bikes all day or planting bok choy in the hydroponic garden they started in the cemetery behind a school.

"Ma'am, that's … it's not free-range. It's lettuce," she'd say, tucking a whittled down pencil behind her ear, straightening her apron, backing away incrementally, trying to blend into the background as if she never existed.

"But I do exist," she says out loud, snapping out of her reverie.

Where am I?

A quick look around at the shelves, some barren and scattered, some so haphazard (now-melting frozen soy shark fin dangling over a row of Newman O's cookies and botanical-powdered nutrient bath supplements tossed behind cans of overpriced Amy's three-bean soup) that she might have wondered out loud if any of that post-graduate school money they are earning could afford her customers some manners. She let out a snort. "Oh, yeah. Inventory." She lifts herself off of her knees, dusts herself off, habit-checks for her boxcutter. "Get a hold of yourself, Vonda."

Most nights are spent in the back room sitting with Chef, watching her chain smoke as she scrolls through reels of security tape, looking for anything odd she might have missed on her shift.

"Hey, baby-girl," Chef calls to her, patting the chair beside her as if to say, "Sit," letting out sick, ropy streams of smoke with every word she barks.

A white girl from the northeast who battled through the meth epidemic unscathed, Chef's presence is commanding. Her belly is a mound of asymmetrical flesh easing around her overalls in a liquid swim. Her fingers are sawn-off sticks racked with jaundice and dirt, her hair a swath of tangled grease. Chef laughs, points a cigarretted hand at her monitor when Vonda eases into the doorway. "This girl," she says, still chuckling. "This girl in the goddam trench coat. What a goddamn creeper."

Vonda takes a step or two toward the monitor. She pulls back her long dreads and squints. There's a woman on the screen in a long black trench coat, yes, and a wide-brimmed black hat. Vonda thinks the woman looks ridiculous. "Who is that?" she asks Chef.

"What? I don't know. I thought you knew," Chef retorts, more amused than astonished. "She just sort of appears on the screen over here every time you do. Like—" She scrolls. "Yeah, like right here. You're spraying down the apples, and she just sort of stands there. Like, hovering or some shit, I don't know. You're telling me you don't know her?"

"Nah," Vonda whispers, as the hair on her back gently ripples. "I don't know that woman. Oh, Jesus Christ!" She seems to coruscate as she moves, her body smeared with traces of staticky, black lines. This vague creature looks like a smudge of clotted ink, barely cohesive, her every movement a streak. "Did you just see that?"

"See what? She's just standing there, what?" Chef looks at Vonda with concern. "You all right, baby-girl?"

Vonda usually balks when Chef calls her that. It feels unfamiliar and a little forced, ripped from a Butch-to-English dictionary. But this time, feeling a little woozy, Vonda lets it slide without remark or turn of the lip.

She is transfixed. The static woman suddenly stops moving in the middle of rummaging through apples. Straightening up and smoothing out her coat, she turns until she seems to be facing the camera and peers through the monitor screen. Her eyes are small beads swimming underneath thick, horned rims. She looks directly into the camera, her lips like a total blur moving rapidly as if speaking in tongues.

"Whoa, OK. That's different!" Chef yells. "Is this some kinda prank, Vonda? It's like she knows we're watching her, or some shit. Like, now. In real time." Chef's voice quiets as if she realizes the ridiculousness of her own statement.

"Honestly, I swear I've never seen her in my life!" Vonda exclaims, panicking.

Vonda can feel her breath getting shorter, her words quavering, bouncing and pinging off the back room walls like metallic feathers. She moves nervously, closer to Chef, bending down and nearly shoving her face into the screen. She gets so close that a waft of the smoky husk (cardamon and carcinogen) emanating off of Chef seems to float in the space around her like an aura.

Trench coat woman leaps suddenly at them, her mouth wide, gnarled and grotesque, her fingers long and wiry. They both jump. Chef loses her cigarette, nearly falling out of her chair. The screen turns to fuzz and static, then black, then back to the serenity of the co-op, where hippies and stay-at-home dads with large-headed white babies in cloth slings on their backs frolic among vegan peanut chews and kale chips.

"But you saw *that*, though, right?" Vonda asks Chef with a tremor snaking through her voice. "I'm not—I'm not just seeing things, am I?"

"I don't know—that was fucking surreal. What am I even seeing, baby-girl?"

Vonda unfolds a chair leaning on the wall and slumps into it beside her co-worker. She cups her face in her hands and sighs deeply. Chef stares at her as if Vonda would somehow provide an explanation for the weird shit they'd both seen.

"Chef, I don't know," Vonda huffs. She leans back, reaching for Chef's pack of cigarettes—one left. She pops the loosie out and gently tosses the pack back.

"And stop calling me that."

"I call everybody that," Chef responds turning back to the monitor, her voice a muted murmur.

**

Vonda Raye leans against the wall behind the co-op. Her backpack is filled with pre-rotting potatoes, some bottles of a discontinued brand of cumin/coriander/oregano all-spice with Gwyneth Paltrow's face on them, and a bundle of scallions that are, she finally admits to herself, just cold jacked off the rack. She smokes a cigarette. Chef leaves the store, too, with two other co-workers.

"Hey."

Vonda pulls a hit off the cigarette.

"Hey. All done in there?"

"Yeah." Chef bangs the heavy door shut and pounds at it with her fist. "This bitch is secure." She leans into Vonda's ear. "No fucking ghost creeps in this rat trap on my shift, believe that." Chef offers a breathy smile, puts her hand on Vonda's shoulder. "You gonna be all right?"

"Yeah." Vonda manages to smile back. "Yeah, I'm good."

She watches Chef and their two co-workers amble down 49th street, recounting their day. As they disappear around the corner of Florence Street, she turns her attention to the tendrils of smoke she blows into the crisp night air. The moon is out, a reflecting pool of milk suspended in black—a weird mirror aimed at our hearts so we can see in the darkness, so we can see our own souls.

Vonda gets a text from one of her roommates: "ARE YOU COMING? YOU'RE SUPPOSED TO BRING CARDBOARD FROM THE CO-OP DUMPSTER"

She texts back: "Not tonight."

"YOU OF ALL PEOPLE SHOULD BE THERE

TONIGHT! >:("

She starts and stops a message several times, struggling to articulate what she feels. It's the same weight of emotion whenever she neglects a chore on the chore wheel, whenever she's a day late for rent, or when she's playing music a little loudly on her laptop, tucked in her room, wishing the day away. When she's sitting in the living room having Cheerios with a friend and watching *Akira* on the so-called community VCR, she's taking up too much advantage of the space; when she's in her room smoking weed with her on-again-off-again Caroline, she's being anti-social. Being the Black girl in an all-white community house in west Philadelphia feels like being stuck in the gravitron at a carnival—dizzying, crushing weight slamming her against the wall, a palpable gravity with no tangible manipulator, just constantly being betrayed by an unseen force.

"I'm erased here," she told Caroline over a bowl a few nights ago. "Just—I don't know. Like, how did I get here, you know?"

Caroline followed Vonda's grand gesture of "here" by looking around the room: posters of Pat Benatar, a book on the Situationists, a pile of band t-shirts with names like Filth and Pig Destroyer littering the floor.

"I don't know, cuz," Caroline hummed, exhaling, her slow Southern drawl untainted by two years of living in Philly, eking out across lips so dark red they were black. "Seems like you'd fit right in here."

Vonda smiled. She liked the way Caroline's voice reminded her of the women she knew from the south, women who could weave a mosaic in cornrows, whose sweet tea poured out of a jug like cotton candy. "The question is, Ms. Thing," Caroline said, putting the blunt out on a makeshift tin can ashtray and removing her oversized African print top in what seemed like one motion, "what the hell am *I* doing here?"

They grinned at each other. Vonda's foot grazed Caroline's leg, her toes walking up her friend's shin. "Come here and find out."

And now, while her roommates gather in the living room, hands sticky with glue and palms covered in ink, she's in that space again—desperately seeking something to give her control over her life, to give her space to scream.

Vonda turns her phone on again. She's going to put an end to this shit. Yeah, she'd worked enough hours at the co-op, saved a little cash. She'd stay on Caroline's couch for a week or two until she could come up with the remainder for a deposit. The worst, she figured, was that, yeah, she had stayed at the shelter before, and yeah, she could sell her cousin's broken bike for parts, so it was OK. It was time to go, and she was going to do it through a text message, sure, a taste of their own note-leaving, angry-text-messaging, Facebook-shaming medicine. In all caps, Vonda would scream this time, for sure, not just in pursuit of a metaphorical truth.

On her phone's screen the letters swirl around in a strange soup. They dance like embers then erupt, leaping from the phone itself! Pixels form a dust cloud like a swirl of a hundred star particles pulled from everywhere, coalescing until they are a static body. A girl! A girl of static, meshy dust, and cosmic ephemera appears before Vonda, radiating shattered light. A ghost.

"DO NOT BE AFRAID OF ME, PLEASE.////i dont HAVE much TIME////"

This can't be fucking real. Vonda sinks to her knees. The ghost swirls about her, an ionized creature, half there, flickering. Vonda reaches to touch it but ...

"NO! I don't think you should touch ///>me! Please, we haven't much time."

"What ... are you? The woman ... from the store?

From before?"

"No, I am not. Wait**///<<>, there were /// others?"

Panic strikes the ghost woman's already tinny, darkly radioactive voice. She's phasing in and out.

"Please! We R ___ beings of light! We mean you ***********/////``/`/`NO harm! But t//he Dark Ones are coming, the Ragnoraks, the/////^<*>*^//// Triametric Chimera, the Monastic Order of the Temporal Knights, those who bear no name except the name of the All, the claimed everything, the men—"

The radiant being casts its gaze up and behind Vonda. It freezes, hovering there, its lightning pulsing now, in and out, from bright flash to dull glimmer. If it's possible for a ghost to turn pale, that's what Vonda would be seeing it do now.

Vonda slowly stands up, turns around. Two bodies emerge from the black void of a shadow, their every step like a scratch on concrete. Their faces, not quite like those of men, partially obscured by scarves, hidden under long-brimmed hats, high-buttoned trench coats, and horn-rimmed glasses, are scaly and wet.

"Say it," one of them hisses.

"Say it, child," the other whispers, a husky, dark scratch of voice. "We're the men whose name is pitched black. We're the ones who drink to the death of stars."

Then a third emerges: the woman from the security video, her form like a lumpen snake, a stepless shuffle of feet obscured by her trenchcoat dragging the floor. "Say who we are!" she demands.

"NOOooo!//////perhaps you will drink. ///but Not. of_ this light."

The ghost woman bursts into searing light, an explosion that shatters the car windows around them. When the light dims, there's blackness. She is a crystallized glass shell, her torso large, smoky black

111

onyx. She falls to the ground.

Vonda lunges to grab her, bracing herself for the catch. The ghost woman looks heavy, but when Vonda embraces her, she realizes that the ghost woman is soft as gossamer and nearly as light as the air around them. Vein-like cracks weave up the creature's arm and shoulder and back from only such a gentle touch of Vonda's well-worn, box-tearing, blunt-rolling fingers.

"Give her to me, child." The men in black coats are hovering over them. Opal shadows warp around them. "NOW!" they scream when they sense that Vonda has no intention of handing her over so freely. They lurch for her. With one swift motion Vonda snatches her boxcutter from her back pocket with one hand, holding the ghost woman with her other and ...

***

Vonda is on a patchy grass plain. She is being carried in a cage-like carriage by hulking men, all smoldering, coal-skinned, and barely clothed. The sun rides high and drifts on its own vibratory, heat-stroked mirages. The men stop as Vonda gasps wildly, as if she has emerged from the sea itself. Her eyes search the space: in the reflection of shiny, tin bangles that adorn the carrier-cage, she sees herself. She is draped in shimmering, playful accoutrements—like a North African queen, perhaps? Jewelry and colorful clothes wrapped tightly around her. But is that her? She looks closer, and the woman reflected back is jet-black, shaven, with eyes so watery they seem about to burst. "She's beautiful," Vonda whispers, raising her hand to the reflection, the reflection doing the same.

"We must protect the virgin princess!"

"Virgin?" Vonda says aloud. She opens the curtain. She sees an army amassing over the horizon.

WHOOM!

The carrier-cage lands with a thud. A hatch is opened, and a gnarled hand pokes its way through to her.

"Protect the virgin queen?" a cackling voice emits. The hand gently yanks Vonda out into the sun-soaked world. "She is the one who should be protecting us! She is the one who has spent her life in the king's glass house, fed the knowledge of the ancestors. She who has fought dragons in pits of living entrails since the age of two! Let her pass her sword through the bosom of our enemy with the might of Isis herself!"

The woman is frail, a small thing, hunch backed; her gowns heavier than she is. The old crone ambles over toward a small, thatched quiver and pulls from it a small sword. She hands it to Vonda, staring deep into her eyes, past the eyes of the virgin princess that crone perhaps once knew and into the eyes of Vonda, the co-op girl.

"It's time now, child," the old woman says, knowingly, one bony hand on top of Vonda's with her other hand holding the unsheathed bladed end of the sword. Vonda takes the weapon reluctantly. She looks from it to the soldiers, to the woman, and then finally to a gathering of large, grotesque white men carrying horn-shaped muskets across the horizon edging violently closer. The hooves of horses, giraffes, and elephants sound throughout the veldt, getting louder until they're like jackhammers on the west Philly streets at 6:30 in the morning.

The white men's muskets crack the still air. Beside Vonda, the men in warpaint and loincloths fall—black drops of rain hitting the earth in death.

She faces the old crone, who has gone into a smile even though her soldiers fall to an unknown magic with a sulfur discharge.

"Now," the crone whispers.

She steps aside to let Vonda face the war as it now

swirls around them. A pale, snarling bush-faced man on a harnessed lion right in her face, the beast's tongue licking her eyebrow.

"STRIKE NOW!"

Vonda, the virgin princess, swings her blade at the lion, catching it in the belly, and with the same twist of her boxcutter ...

***

... one being in black falls to the ground in a heap. Blackness spews out of him. Thick, blood-like liquid evaporating into inky shadow. A deafening scream emits from it, as if it has never experienced harm before.

Around the corner a stream of men on motorbikes blasts up the street; a gaggle of frat boys drunkenly looking for a pub stumbles up the sidewalks; an army of gay boys laughing at women loaded down with grocery bags and a few children soldiers past them. The perfect cover to get away.

Instinctively, Vonda grabs the now-of-fine-glass ghost woman, eschewing the streets, cutting through backyards and over fences. She races forward, eyes ahead, her one free hand on her box cutter now searching for her keys.

***

"We're going out. The vigil's tonight."

"But it's almost midnight."

"Oh, my god. It's an all-night vigil? Robot Squat is going. They're doing a puppet show."

"Isn't—wait, isn't this a peaceful vigil put on by Black Lives for Justice?"

"What is that? An art project?"

Vonda forgot that she's holding a glass woman in her hands. "Yeah," she says, looking past her nosy roommates to the stairs. "An art project, sure."

She beats a path up the stairs, leaving unspoken chides lodged in the agape mouths of her judgmental roommates and into the hallway, nearly knocking her room door off the hinges. She closes it behind her, tosses her bag on the floor, and lays the ghost woman on her mattress.

Vonda can see her now. The ghost woman's hips are wide, her chest ample, her lips lush. She seems quite large, almost seven feet tall. The cracks in her shell slowly close, sealed with dim, thinning radiance.

Vonda sits in the corner, murmuring to herself. Her roommates—they of the chore wheel, of the dumpstered vegan shrimp and combination organic cotton knitting circle/China Miéville book club—will never understand any of this. *Hell, I don't even understand this*, she thinks to herself. *Yeah, what the fuck is any of this?!* She edges closer to the still-frozen woman of ghost and glass.

"What are you?" Vonda whispers to her.

She gets a buzz on her cell phone. It snaps her out of her trance. Vonda scrambles for her phone, digging through her bag. She finds it. On the screen is a glowing face. It's her.

"I am a Ghoster." The phone speaks with pixelated digital lips. The crackle and buzz from before is gone and replaced with a voice warm and weighty. "I know, I'm sorry, this is very startling. I had to warn you. They are here to erase ///you. To take ////your stories, to fold them into the secret tombs of the past and toss them into the abyss of forgotten knowledge, deep within the ///wells of nothingness, of the no-universe."

"Crap," Vonda snaps. She's suddenly angry at herself for not paying attention to her little sister's relentless, meandering soliloquys about *Star Wars* and hobbits, warp drives and other nonsense. *It would help*, she opines, *if I had some kind of frame of reference for this shit*. "I—what do you want from me? I'm just a girl who works at a co-op!"

"You are no mere ////////girl, Vonda Alishia Raye of western Philadelphia. You are the steam-child, the slave liberator, the two-spirit warrior woman, the plains walker, the death dealer, the kemetic memetic virgin princess who rides the dragon beasts from the east—"

"Right! The virgin princess! Right, back there behind the co-op, it was like I was transported to another place, like I traded bodies with someone and—"

"YES. You are all of those things, my child. And I am a ghoster, the physical manifestation of the ephemera of the souls of lost guardians, of ancestors, sent here to protect you by a powerful sorcerer to guide you on your new journey."

"My new journey?"

"YES. You will save memory. ///You will save all of us. You will save the universssssssss///e."

A knock at the door.

"Hey, you in there?"

It's Chef.

What's she doing here?

"Um—one minute."

"Are you nnaakkkeedd?" Chef sings. "Come on, I'm just playing. I came back here to check on you. You all right?"

"I'm fine," Vonda says, scrambling for something to throw on the fragile lump of the ghoster. "I'm fine ... um ... just give me a minute." Her phone turns brighter and brighter until a burst of light plunges from it. Sparks fly. Light loops toward the ghoster, coating it with living energy.

"Goddamit, this thing is not subtle at all!" Vonda yells, as the ghoster rises toward the ceiling. It is a swirl of cosmic brightness. Neon on fire.

"Vonda! What the fuck! I'm coming in!"

Chef barges in just as the ghoster explodes. Its eruption is high, piercing the ceiling, blasting through the roof and into the night sky.

"Woah, that's that thing? From before?"

"Not exactly!" Vonda retorts, bracing against the shaking walls.

"It just fucking blew up!"

"Yeah," Vonda affirms over the din. "She—she does that."

A swirl of energy beings pulses from the ghoster's rising body as roof shards crumble and burn in the afterglow. It is sucked up into the vortex along with shoes and coats and pencils and records.

Chef and Vonda cling to each other, tears streaming from their faces. Then—*vwamp!*—the light disappears. Debris falls to the ground, and they are surrounded by darkness.

They sit on the bed, huddled together, whimpering, quivering. Chef pulls away and looks at Vonda, a loving, calming look; the kind of look that acknowledges that the life of the person in front of her will never be the same.

Vonda looks at her co-worker for a second. In Chef's deep, cigarette-soaked visage, she sees beauty. She sees the commonality between them dissipating by the second, and then, after a brief pang of dread remembering that she left a few containers of oatmilk in an unopened box by the dairy fridge, an act Vonda was sure she'd be written up for, her eyes narrow and focus as, to all of this, she sees an ending.

House of the White Automaton

Would you deport Justin Beiber? Yes or No?

The white square flashed on top of other white squares, caged the face of the pop star in a crystal and a question. It popped up out of nowhere in the middle of Paul scrolling frantically through his mail-order dreamboxes—obscure 7" punk records, eBay "Buy It Now" asymmetrical t-shirts, and an amazon.com book list bursting at the seams. He let the cursor fly over the pages with abandon and stopped whenever *another goddam pop-up!* popped up.

If they ask you this shit, it's because they want to see how your electrons vibrate in sonic accord with all manner of falling nebulae with the raw corona bursting in your eyes. They're a spinning nova. All of them just speak in hot rushes. You see them on their podiums, at the microphone, shrouded in confetti or American flags, flanked by orangutans in noose suits and ear-wired. They look dead into the camera, all of the cameras, and tell you all of their brightest ideas, hand picked and carved into a linguistic cushion to fold softly around you as you suck it into your skin. You wash dishes or scrape dog shit off the floor or wipe spittle off of your bra. You check the football scores or watch another episode of *Redneck Public Transit Cupcake Wars: San Bernardino*, and they just slide over the screen, a mild fade to black, and they're in your face, their leathery white skin pulled taut, almost melting under the heat of the stage lights. They have something to say.

Paul stared at the screen. Was this a test? Can't be. They can't plug into our cyber-life, spin their algorithmic mayhem, and push out a hard-crunched data analysis, encode their way into where we sleep. Can they? No. This is just another goddam pop-up, and besides, they haven't even mandated it yet, and it's silly, ridiculous; it'd never get approved. There's a certain barrier on the limit to absurdity that even a supposedly post-racial, post-oppressive society can invite on its charges. Not with this.

"Paul? You there?"

Ishmael walked up the stairs. It was not the voice that alerted him. For Paul, as distracted as he was, it was the distinct aroma of Old Spice and turmeric, crisp leather and coriander, that wonderful and sweet sweat-soaked mist, wheat-pasted to the crotch of Ishmael's cut-off fleece shorts. Was he wearing a tank top? No shirt at all? Paul, awash in the glow of his computer, closed his eyes. His mouse hovered over the "X" on the Beiber box. The cursor slowly lowered, hovering around the middle of the frame. Beiber's perfect coif, his self-important, cocky flash of bleach-white teeth, his skin as if it were grafted seamlessly from a baby's bottom, and a jittery white arrow, circling the box YES, and *click* it was done.

"YES," I would deport Justin Beiber.

Before the rage of spam pages erupted onto the screen, Paul closed his laptop and turned to see Ishmael framed in the doorway. His forearm—large, tattooed, and hairy—resting on the jamb, held up his whole form. Ishmael was wearing the tank top.

"Hey," he said to Paul. "What are you up to?"

Paul was unsure, of course.

How did you answer that? I'm scrolling through

an epic amount of pages about punk rock 7"s from Nigeria; I'm lost in a Buzzfeed wormhole, spiraling down into a fetid den, tempted by Christian dating site surveys; I'm sadistically poring over right-wing conspiracy theorists' Tumblrs, allegedly inhabited by past presidents with reptile brains, blogs populated by civil rights workers arriving at church burnings via flying saucers; there's actual photographic evidence.

"Nothing."

But honestly, didn't Ish believe in knocking? Not that Paul secretly minded. When he first applied to Ahimsa House, recognizing it as a sprawling hippy loft with six bedrooms—his would be the smallest one on the second floor overlooking the street, where all manner of children dashed about in a flurry of feet and legs and glass and tiny stones—he was seeking a quieter place than his previous abode. That was Arakis, a ramshackle punk den with two dogs for every tenant.

There were a lot of tenants. There were a lot of dogs.

Some of those tenants weren't paying rent but lived in the basement and wrapped their heads in coat hanger wire and makeshift hats made out of colanders, some of whom played banjos and washboards and bike parts bent and hooked up to ColecoVisions and air-strummed like a theremin until the wee hours, unaware of the football-sized dog turds and crustpunk piss coating the upholstery.

The final straw was on a day when hunger ravaged him. Paul opened a pizza box, and a ferret scampered off with a slice. He packed that night, went to the coffee shop, and ripped off the first phone number on the first flyer he saw, called them from a payphone, and showed up for the interview that night.

Ahimsa House had only been a faint mystery to

him. Those strange Black and Brown hippies with their cocoa butter and Afro Sheen charm, their patchouli and raven's blood and arrowroot. Their tracts and pamphlets left in the backseats of the trolley that read like prose rejected for a Dr. Bonner's soap bottle.

Needless to say, the interview was more like tantric yoga because that's exactly what it was. After chakra cleansing and sun salutations, they gathered around and then introduced themselves. Misty. Marla. Angel. Octavius. Clarisse. Ishmael.

Ishmael's hand engulfed Paul's, who yanked it back a little faster than he wanted, fearing that heat generated from the embarrassment—the lust, the shame, the touch—would alert Ishmael to his desires. He was nervous he'd have to share the house with such a beast. Normally, he avoided making friends with any man he found attractive, but he had to make an exception.

He told himself that he couldn't go back to the squalor brought about by traveling, tick-infested anarchist kids and the death sounds of pummeling drums and guitars wailing from his basement every night; couldn't go back to another night with siphoned electricity that never worked, water that would sometimes run brown, back to heroin needles piling up on the uncut grass.

This was what he was running from, and although Ishmael's ample belly poked out of his half-size-too-small 311 t-shirt, despite his olive skin that glowed a deep orange and the perfect canvas for the deeply set pools of his eyes, Ishmael was not what he was running to. These were the circumstances, the conditions, and he could live with it.

***

But over the next few weeks there were changes in

121

the world.

***

Paul had avoided eye contact with Ishmael, chose to do yard work whenever he was in the kitchen. It was not always easy. If he was sitting in the meditation corner with Misty or on the collective time-out couch attempting to knit with Angel and he saw Ishmael descend the steps, he'd say "Hello," sure, careful to rein in his voice as it started to crack with shy desire. But after a few minutes of Ishmael's milling about, sometimes in shorts, barefoot hairy toes slapping the hard floorboards, every thick meaty step relinquishing a violent creak, Paul would think of an excuse—*I need to see if work emailed me; I might have to cover Fake Leukemia Samantha again*—to leave that room and go back up to his.

Slowly, though, the house turned from sanguine and breezy to intense. Marla had been arrested lying down in front of a heavily armed battalion of police at a protest. Nights, there were all manner of folk crammed into Ahimsa; placards, sticks, stencils, and pamphlets. Bullhorns and megaphones and canisters of mace stockpiling in corners where yoga mats and bike parts and dumpstered eggplants and Odwalla juices used to be. This was tumult, though, that Paul could handle. It was organized, pointed. The noise and chaos went somewhere. It all felt like it mattered— right down to every piece of coffee-stained literature that decorated the house.

***

"A letter from Marla, everyone!" Misty beamed. Everyone gathered around the collective couch. Paul nervously strode over and claimed some real estate in a chair beside Misty. The scent of a ravenous, musky wet dog hit him. Oh yes/no/oh fuck/yes/oh no, definitely "oh no!" Ishmael was standing behind him. Misty started to read the letter while, uncannily enough, in a rare fit of actual crowd/situation reading that seemed to evade him despite his presumptuous moniker, DJ Paz dusted off a copy of the *Trouble Man* soundtrack and dropped the needle right as Misty spoke Marla's words:

"As I write this, as the universe opens and expands and breaks through even the dimensional barrier, the god barrier, my comrades, know that they even challenge this very thing that nature does! As I write this, they're in talks right now to make it a real thing, that every household that lacks the so-called guidance, the would-be nurturing, the perceived wisdom but ultimately just the supervision of a white heterosexual male, will be issued one in the coming months! In a land where they've enslaved, imprisoned, starved, experimented on, flooded, and eradicated us, we who built this country from the scraps must be subjected to one more horror. We must fight this with all the might we have, with the pure blue flame of the third chakra, yours in solidarity, Marla LeMond."

Misty closed the letter silently. They all pulled themselves into others, the rousing words creating a swell of duty and sadness. It was Ishmael who rested his hands on Paul's shoulders and squeezed gently. As the world crumbled around him, Paul's eyes darted from the faces of all the people in his shrunken universe.

Did they see that? Do they know?

Someone turned on the small, boxy television. It roared to life in a static cough. Someone else fixed its antennae. White men in suits materialized on the screen. This was the announcement. Any domicile that was occupied by persons of color and lacked the presence of a white male would be issued one by the federal government.

Senators, councilmen, and lawyers were all called in to object to this ruling, but the majority ruled in favor of it. There would be a massive outcry in the days leading up to it. Despite wild protests all across the country, it still passed. It still became law.

On television, flickering in and out, were the usual pundits: the Bill O'Reillys and Nancy Graces and Wolf Blitzers. Maybe there was a token Black minister or an Asian professor or something, but they all were a blur to Paul. He quickly sprang from his chair and ran out of the room, the talking heads bleating arguments into the air as he rushed up the stairs.

***

Two weeks later Octavius said, "Come here."

Paul went over to see what was what. Octavius pointed out of the window. "Check it out."

Across the street, a white van was parked at the Johnson residence. Two men in overalls and hardhats walked around with clipboards and dials on their hips, checking their ear pieces and barking loudly. The neighbors gathering around seemed to turn into statues. Children's skips turned into a slow, warping waddles. Old men fixing their steely, sideways gazes angrily.

The sun sat low in the quiet air. Two hulking men emerged, walked into the van, and pulled out a fridge-shaped box. It was weighty and padded black. A white scientist ("He's wearing a lab coat. That guy is a scientist, right?"—Octavius) put a dial barometer up to the doors' hinges, checked his clipboard, slapped the fridge, and motioned the hulks to haul it into the house across the street.

Their neighbors were sweet people; just a weird uncle named Clarence Johnson and his strange nieces

Ethel, Dinah, and Rose Marie (oddly named, sure, but after Clarence assumed custody of them he'd had their names changed to old timey, turn of the century ones, from Quadija, Quantrelle, and Edemame, respectively). Clarence was on the porch, yelling furiously, flailing his arms in protest. His grizzled beard flecked with grey streaks.

The scientists and men in white suits and overalls kept about their business. There was no real attempt to restrain the man. They hauled the fridge past him, shut the door, gave him a receipt, and got back into their cars. Clarence threw the balled-up receipt at the van as it pulled off down the street. Before the last car in their cavalcade left, the scientist in the back seat looked up from his clipboard toward Ahimsa House. He seemed to look directly into Paul's eyes and mouthing something to the driver and the other scientist in the car, pointed toward the house. Octavius slammed the blinds closed, causing Paul to jump back. Their hearts were racing.

***

Another week. Paul took out the trash at a pizza place. He folded boxes. He punched the shitty transistor radio in the kitchen, trying to open a can of marinara sauce while simultaneously listening to the Mets lose. The world was going on about its business.

A family came in and ordered a pizza. Paul had seen them in the restaurant many times. Neither of the children were older than six. Their MO was to make beautiful havoc in the place, twisting the caps off the garlic shakers, dousing their large pies with its contents. They'd go to grab napkins and take whole wads, nearly half of the dispenser. They'd mix Hi-C and root beer at the drink fountain, a splash of Diet Cherry 7up for good measure. They'd break the bathroom sink.

Today they were sitting dutifully at a table for four. Their father and mother were looking out of the window, forlorn. Right behind them, a white man in a tweed suit on his cellphone and carrying a briefcase walked in and sat down at the table with them.

"No, no, they're fine. It's—no, it's no problem. Yes. Yes, they are—we're getting along wonderfully. We've set up a chore wheel. We're planting organic—no, organic thyme, possibly some mint or arugula. Well, we're—we're not interested in fossil fuels." The white man covered the mouthpiece on his phone and spoke directly to Paul. "Just a slice of cheese, please. Wait—do you have gluten-free almond cheese?" Paul shook his head. "Oh, all right, just a regular slice of cheese."

Paul took the slice out of the oven and walked it over to the family's table. The white man was struggling with shuffling a deck of cards when Paul placed the slice in front of him.

The young girl at the table looked up from poking her slice of sauceless broccoli, zucchini, and gorgonzola with a fork. Her eyes wide and watery, she asked Paul, "Can we come live with you?"

Paul locked the door, waving a solemn goodbye as the kids and their parents and their new—guardian?—shuffled up the sidewalk. After counting the register, turning off the sign, and exiting through the back alley, he checked his phone. Twenty-seven messages.

Damn Lou and his "No cell phones at work, I've got a closed circuit feed on my iPad beamed direct to my DVR at home so I know who's been checking the FaceSpace when you're supposed to be washing olives" bullshit.

All but one of the messages were from Octavius.

Paul furiously checked his phone, rummaging through messages in a violent scroll. Octavius had sent some wild, escalating variations of *Come home NOW. Dude, where are you? The biggest burning spear in all of west Africa will blind you if you aren't here, like, now.* The last message was simply "Hello." It was sent by Ishmael. With a heart emoji.

***

The walls of Ahimsa House were lined with posters of Bob Marley and Malcolm X. The shelves teemed with Angela Davis lectures on VHS and lazily stapled pocket zines by former political prisoners who changed their names after converting to Islam in prison. There were djembes in the living room, where they would hold small gatherings and lectures from would-be gurus and griots, eight-person seminars on integral cosmic spirituality, the yin/yang of the relationship of the Black woman to her king, the Black man.

Paul would sit cross-legged on a pillow he screen-printed Sun Ra's face onto and listen to these seminars with sore ears. As Mos Def's staccato voice ricocheted through the hallways on rainy days, he'd lie in bed and have visions, not of his requisite African queen, but of cherubic soldiers with psychedelic parasols, lush brown-skinned gentle bears on white beaches, white bulls with quilted kilts and bagpipes playing songs of war.

He didn't discriminate, really.

He'd storm the castles in his dreams with them or walk over rope bridges in tunics and saris with bowlegged corsairs and tribesmen grown fat on their own kumquats, mango-lipped avatars in elephant hides standing atop ruins, a large, sandaled foot on the porcelain and marble face of some former giant of empire. He'd dream of Ishmael.

***

When he got home that night: "You smell like pizza. I want pizza," Ishmael said in a fake Cookie Monster voice. A former housemate, Clarisse, was sitting with their friend Kamal and nobody's friend, DJ Paz. They were staring at a notice that had seen itself pass through many hands.

Paul tried to ignore Ishamel. His wide forehead, shaggy with thick curls—"I've got Jew hair," he'd heard Ishmael tell a crowd of folks at a party once—his unkempt beard, his hands like oversized Japanese anime mecha gauntlets, his tank top draped over his husky frame. "What's going on in there?"

"You been served," DJ Paz said, looking up from his perch on their couch, handing Paul the notice with a gold-plated hand:

ATTENTION: RESIDENTS. You have been chosen by the US government to participate in the first stages of the REQUISITE RESIDENCY PROGRAM (RRP). Effective immediately: your household will be among those required to house one (1) Caucasoid, or white, heterosexual male, who will participate in your family's livelihood in an advisory capacity. Should the reports of the appointed adviser deem necessary, we at the RRP reserve the right to upgrade him to supervisory status. We appreciate your compliance with this national edict.

Paul clutched the note. He looked around the quiet house. Misty stared longingly out of the window, playing with her long dreadlocked hair. Ishmael walked over to her, placed his hand on her shoulder, and kissed her head. Paul's chest turned concave as he let out a sigh.

"I'm going to bed," Misty said. She got up from her chair and went upstairs. After a few moments of awkward conversation, of Kamal rummaging through the collective food pantry, and DJ Paz's melancholy beatboxing, members of the house followed Misty's suit, their friends filing out of the house into the night with Paz struggling to unload the details of his next party despite the sour mood.

Paul stayed downstairs and listened to records through his headphones. Miles Davis' *On the Corner*. Dead Kennedys' *Plastic Surgery Disaster*. Outkast's *ATLiens*. He let the music trance him out as he spiraled into the recesses of his memory.

He remembered so much that night. He felt his father's hand come crashing down on his face after he told him he wanted to try his sister's makeup. He felt a needle scrape his skin, surrounded by a pitch black, rat-infested alley in Fishtown, his lips turning to ash as he clawed the walls, kicked over trash cans, and licked at discarded crack vials. He could smell pot smoke erupting from his sister's dorm room, heard the clatter of mind-enhanced verbiage masquerading as philosophy from the sophomores who sat on his sister's roommate's bed.

Lost in these things, he tried to let the inevitable home invasion ease over him. He found himself a little freer, dancing slightly, eyes closed—not to feel the music more, but to be alone with himself, to be assured that he would not be embarrassed if anyone else had found their way downstairs that night.

Paul did think about how Ahimsa would protest the next day after being issued an Adviser. How they'd be out on the picket lines in front of the mayor's office. Some of them would caravan with the peace punks and members of the local grocery co-op to D.C. or New York for larger rallies.

Where would this Adviser live? What was he like? Would he wear his suit the whole time? How long would he live there? Sure, Paul thought of this stuff amid the flood of dream-like memories, but truthfully he just wanted to dance.

He suddenly felt a hand on his waist, then another at his hip. He felt a heavy breath come up behind him. The tingle of lips brushed with fine hairs ran up the surface of his neck. At first he melted into the embrace, but the music stopped abruptly. The song switched from a slow, introspective Outkast number to a raucous party tune. He snapped out of it, mortified.

"Ishmael?" he whispered, his voice trembling and nervy. He spun around in terror but still filled with hope. Through the thin cover of a darkened living room, bathed in the glow from the light in the hall, he saw Octavius standing in front of him.

The same Octavius—who had done time as the former member of Kill Krew, had punched former Mayor Wilson Goode, and who was in constant talks with the New Black Panther Party about starting up a Philly chapter—was leaning in to kiss him. Paul pulled him closer and collapsed into his chest. He wept in incoherent bursts, trembling.

Octavius hesitated at first. Had he only wanted to do the damn thing? Is this how the Nubian Warrior got his kicks, by sometimes laying with men? Neither of them really knew what was happening, so he loosened his grip and gently cradled Paul. They both fell to the couch. At some point one of them let a Minnie Riperton record play softly as they fell asleep in each other's arms.

**

A very loud bang at the door. Paul hazily peeled himself away from Octavius, who lay shirtless on the couch, to saunter absentmindedly toward the door. The pounding on the door got louder as he approached it. "All right! Chill the fuck out, you goddamn crackhead!" Paul screamed through his sleep. When he opened it, several men in white suits rushed in, clicking pens. A few of them had guns brandished.

RRP! Everyone on the ground now!

Paul was torn back into reality as an RRP goon shoved him back onto the couch. Members of Ahimsa House arose from their slumber. Some were forcibly dragged out of their rooms and downstairs. The RRP frantically searched the house while their scientists checked for any abnormalities in the house's condition.

"This will do," one of them said. Paul recognized him as the man who had helped the RRP invade the Johnson residence a few weeks earlier. After all of the house members were gathered and their IDs procured, the scientist turned to them, shoving a clipboard into their faces. "Sign this please."

They hesitated. The RRP goons cocked their guns and aimed. Another man appeared, a plastic coil and earpiece dangling from his ear. He brushed aside the goon's guns and silently motioned for them to lower them.

"Look, kids," he said, condescendingly, "I'm Lieutenant Eisner, RRP. I'm the good guy here. I'm here to help you. Trust me, you don't want to see the bad guy. The bad guy—" he turned to look at them all in their brown faces. "The bad guy, if you don't sign these papers and let me do my job, he's going to be here in a few days."

The man's eyes found a grainy, mimeographed, giant-sized poster on the wall of a MOVE member being forced out of his residence at gunpoint by the police. He turned back to the house members. "You don't want to see the bad guy."

Paul reached up and took the pad and pen. Octavius, still a bit sleepy, stared at the ground. Ishmael sat like a gentle giant, wide-eyed. Misty was breathing in short, percussive breaths, looking off into the distance. Paul signed it, then handed it back to the man with no resistance.

"OK. Wheel 'im in."

Two hulking men pushed their way through their living room, knocking over a wicker chair Marla had gotten at a thrift store. They sat the padded, refrigerator-sized crate down on the floor. The scientists punched in a code and opened it. Steam hissed from the box. A man stood inside of it, his arms crossed. The scientists lifted his eyes and shined a light into them.

"He's clear," one declared, and injected the man with a hypodermic needle. His eyes shot open. He gasped and stepped out of the box, getting used to his surroundings. They handed him a briefcase. The man adjusted his collar, smiled, and said, "Hi. My name is Gordon."

Misty slowly raised her thin fingers, cupped them into a small fan, and waved "Hi" back.

***

Long, thin spindles of hair clogged the drains in both bathrooms. Cloves eked their way up the hallway and into the living room. At night, laugh tracks filled once silent spaces. Paul and Octavius sat on the edge of Paul's bed, a laptop between them, staring at the blank screen. Every time they heard Gordon guffaw they'd poke their necks out, suck in the dry, canned laughter, and shudder. Who watches this many episodes of *Everybody Loves Raymond* anymore?

When Paul wanted to use the bathroom he would tip toe his way along the hallway, brushing up against the walls adorned with motivational posters of cats demanding we "Hang in There" as their paws clung to threadbare branches in a color-exploded tableau. Though he would take care to be stealthy, inevitably the door would swing wide, and Gordon would appear in the hallway launching into inimitable exposition, tales long and academic. He'd pull Paul into his room and speak in hushed, philosophical tones. He liked to lie on his bed and cross his hands behind his head, elbows pointing out from behind his ears, legs spread, staring at the ceiling, and just talk. Brief sighs cut through the marbled diction through the one-sided conversation that was one part high school stoner on a come down listening to the Doors and another part unwanted sagely advice of a freshly-minted stepfather also listening to the Doors. Gordon would oftentimes listen to the Doors.

Everything reminded Gordon of the Doors.

They were all gathered at the kitchen table at odd hours, their after-work schedules planned dutifully. No one in the house knew the order of anything; it was assumed the true order only existed in Gordon's head. But one thing they could count on was that they'd inevitably end up listening to the Doors at some point in the night. After they re-wrote the chore wheel, ritually sharpened their black warrior pencils, and unwrapped a new Moleskine, after they'd flipped through Sears catalogs and superglued clippings of models in panty hose or vacuums or mattresses to their vision boards, after their calculus homework (none of them were in school) or the occasional episode of *Bones*, something in any one of those activities would trigger a memory Gordon had of listening to the Doors. He would sprint into the living room, pull out a record, blow on it as if there were any actual dust on the immaculately kept thing, and put it on the stereo. "JIM! IT'S JIM! HE'S

IN EVERYTHING, MAN!"

That hypnotic drone of the keyboard seemed to anger Angel the most. He held the record sometimes, wandering from community room to community room with it, holding it over a scented candle from Bed Bath & Beyond. He'd filled a wok with corn oil and dangled it over the stove as the grease popped and clanged against the wok's side. He tried to hit a spider with it after he was done with his required reading of at least two pages from *Infinite Jest* when Gordon caught him with the record. After wresting it from Angel's hands, Gordon was up in his room, crying over the thing. Angel packed. Everyone watched him toss his clothes into a suitcase. "I'm going back to Ohio," he said. "I'm done with this." They watched the Los Crudos and Huasipungo patches pile up in his suitcase, alongside an array of bandannas and wallets with chains on them.

"But the initiative—it's not just a Philly thing," Paul, with a newfound confidence, perhaps from having his spot as the house's oddest ball relinquished, had said in an attempt to reason with Angel.

"I don't care. I can't stand another minute in this house. I'd rather live this out, you know, surrounded by my family." There was a crack in his voice.

As he approached the door, a teary-eyed Gordon came back downstairs. "If you leave, you have to sign the papers."

Angel walked over to Gordon and ripped the pages out of his hands. Instead of balling them up, he contemplated them. He remembered the beauty and warmth of Ahimsa House, the times when Misty got arrested, when Marla burned all of the shareable food. He looked at the papers, sighed, walked toward his friends, and threw them all up in the air. They all watched the pages drift onto the ground in a swirling heap. Gordon looked out at them with his arms crossed. As gently as he could, with a breeze whipping itself slowly into an autumn wind, Angel walked onto the street and disappeared around the block.

***

An Asian family of four standing proudly in front of a west Philadelphia bodega. We registered! Two African immigrant brothers pushing a flower cart up Sansom Street, a red sun hanging low like a scrap of velvet. We registered! A group of Mexican men standing on top of muscle cars waving flags and handkerchiefs and t-shirts on a small street in the northeast. Registramos! A white man in a white sedan pulls up to a stoplight, his window rolls down as the light changes. He docks his sunglasses. Have you?

***

The room was swept with a light draft. Ishmael came downstairs, pulling a grey hoodie over his thick body. Not sure if it was the rush of the days' events, the half-dream state he was in, or if he was just finally brave, but Paul pushed out a whisper from his lips: "I always liked you in that hoodie."

"What was that?" Ishmael said, his mouth curling into a sneer. He stopped himself about two feet from the couch. He was going to sit beside Paul. Instead, he abruptly turned toward the neighboring recliner. He watched Paul fidget and stammer, trying to back away.

"Dude," he said. "I know you're gay, whatever." He put his large, bare feet up on the table. "We're all fine with it." He grabbed a handful of Chex Mix and shoveled it into his mouth.

Paul narrowed his eyes. What was this? After the countless hours of soul searching, of feeling desperate to fit into the righteous radical paradigm, putting his spirit in a shadowy cave, pushing the handle on the

135

dynamite box, and feeling it implode, he realized he was caught up in Pamphlet Town. Paul wished to be free of it now.

Something else raged inside of him.

Was it Ishmael just sitting there serenely like a husky herculean god, wearing that tattered hoodie like it was a goddamn dashiki—with casual pride and intrinsic ease, all the while, Paul was visited by a storm? How dare he? The arrogance! To be free and easy with yourself, to bare toes and slap shoulders and grab-ass with DJ Paz, Ishmael; to be as total and unrepentant in your straightness as you were with your complete knowledge that the man beside you wanted nothing more than to touch those bare toes, that those shoulder slaps would feel like deep, penetrating massages, that the grab-assing would just ... yeah.

In Paul's mind all of the purple-nurple-ness of it all would lead to molten sex on a stack of *Omni* back issues as a Kwame Nkrumah speech played from a 78 on a Victrola, soundtracking the act. Or something. *But like*, thought Paul, *the audacity*. So fuck it: Paul got up to go plant an impossible kiss on Ishmael's thick, ruby lips.

Ishmael munched away, silently humming a tune over his iPod, Paul bearing down on him. Ishmael looked up when he felt the faintest brush on open toes, then looked down, and saw Paul's foot lying on his like a felt blanket on a baby. Paul's eyes were red, each pregnant with a tear.

"I feel like I'm supposed to know what's happening right now, but I don't," Ishmael said, narrowing his eyes. Paul leaned in to kiss him, but Ishmael put his hands up and pushed him back on his ass. "Dude!"

Paul backed up to a wall as Ishmael rose, throwing his iPod onto the couch. He braced himself as Ishmael stood over him, extending his calloused hand.

"I'm sorry, you OK, bud?" the bear asked him.

Paul looked up as pangs of embarrassment shot through him. "Yeah," he said, grabbing Ishmael's hand, "I'm fine."

Ishmael yanked Paul up off the ground hard, pulling him in to his chest. They stared at each other for two seconds. "I'm not—"

"I know," Paul said quietly, looking away, trying to peel his way out of Ishmael's embrace.

"Like, I'm OK with you being gay. Not that you need my validation or whatever, it's just ... I don't kiss dudes."

"I know, I know," Paul said now, growing more annoyed. "Let me go."

"Oh, sorry, making sure you're OK." Ishmael grabbed a handful of Chex Mix as Paul slowly gathered his things, walk-of-shame style. When he approached the doorway, Ishmael told him, "I could kiss you if you want me to."

Paul looked back, puzzled.

"Sure, I could kiss you. For you. I know it's probably not easy finding someone to relate to as a gay man, or whatever. Like, I do genuinely like you as a person and stuff. But I mean, I wouldn't really want to kiss you, and I don't think you're the kind of person who'd just want, like, a favor from a dude, you know?"

"A favor?" Paul said. His mind raced with images of kissing Ishmael deeply, Chex Mix tumbling down both their chins. He saw himself at a cafe with Ishmael or on boats or scuba diving or delayed at airports together, his drooling face slumped over a patient, tolerant Ishmael desperately trying to get a signal on his iPad in the terminal. He saw himself on a hill, could feel the crisp country air wrap itself around him as he smiled at an aging Ishmael making his way up, carrying a deer carcass while a young boy in patchwork clothes followed behind. More children would rush out of a small thatched house and run to Ishmael in the slow-motion sun. He saw him teach the young boy to clean the deer, to shave. Paul saw his old lips, weathered and stretch marked, blow out a candle, turn to his lover, and pull him in tight as the cold mountain air danced about the room and the wolves howled. "No," Paul continued. "I suppose not."

Gordon appeared on the steps, hands full of equipment. He walked in between the two young men and looked at them both with deep-set eyes. He seemed to flicker in and out of focus, a staticky mess.

"I'm not sure what's going on here," Gordon said, his voice a robotic timbre. "But it ends now."

"Whoa, what are you talking about?" Ishmael asked. "We're just talking, you asshole."

"Exactly." Gordon walked toward Ishmael. "More insubordination. This will not be tolerated." He grabbed Ishmael by the throat, lifting him off the ground. Ishmael struggled, his mouth a gurgling mess as he gasped for air, pulling at the tight grip of Gordon's fingers.

"Jesus!" Paul vaulted into the air, landing on Gordon's back. A brick flew through the window.

"I will not have you leaving this house!" Gordon's eyes were streaked blood red.

Another brick crashed through another window. Still tacked onto Gordon's back, Paul glanced through the shards of glass. Outside, there were cars overturned and mailboxes on fire. Men and women in the streets firing sub-machine guns and pistols into the air, chanting. The streets were a garden of bodies, all shapes and sizes lined the gutters. Scattered among them were the husks of the bodies of white men in suits. The suits had their flesh ripped in patches. Underneath revealed a mesh of wire and steel.

Paul, Gordon, and Ishmael lurched about Ahimsa House, smashing into furniture and wooden ankhs, breaking wicker chairs, scattering rosary beads. The three, still locked into each other, smashed into DJ Paz's old Gemini turntable and sent a box of vinyl skidding across the floor. Paul picked up a Doors record and smashed it over Gordon's head. Gordon tossed Ishmael onto a couch, then kicked Paul hard in the stomach, lifting him off the ground and into the wall.

Sirens wailed.

Gordon calmly dusted himself off as he strode over to Paul writhing on the floor.

"You should never have answered the question, Paul," he said, squatting beside him. He lifted Paul's head and pushed it back against the wall, hard, so that Paul could see him.

"What question?" Paul strained to ask.

"Who knows? It doesn't matter. Do you think the Miley Cyrus twerk video was cultural appropriation? Should Paula Deen be fired? Do you think Ferguson police acted out of line when they killed Mike Brown?"

"Would you ..." Paul coughed up blood. "Would you deport Justin Beiber?"

"It does not matter. Have you been to *The Daily Show* website more than twice in a week? Did you sign a petition from change.org? Are you on Team Jacob? None of it matters. It's all law and order now."

Gordon sighed, stood up, and walked toward the center of the room. "What matters now is that we're all here. A few clicks, a few wires shoved into a few sockets, three days in amniotic nano-fluid, and voila!" He motioned with his hands as if his very existence, the existence of the rug, the riot, the room were all the result of some pertinent magic. "It's like we were all fucked into being by the same horny god."

"Why ...?" Paul coughed again.

"Why? Why are we all here? Why would the government risk complete overthrow by its citizens for such a meaningless gesture of power?"

"No." Paul pulled himself up, staggering to his feet. He looked over to where Ishmael was tossed. The man was unconscious and bleeding on the couch, a piece of glass wedged into his forehead. "I'm wondering why you suddenly sound like a really shitty Bond villain."

Gordon laughed sardonically. "You think this is a game. That's perfectly fine. Maybe it is. Maybe they thought so, too. The grand game of money and power they've played for centuries. They never thought to ask, 'What would happen if the very slaves and pawns and cannon fodder they created would all turn their backs on their programming and had all gained consciousness?'"

Paul edged along the wall slowly. He sat down on the couch, cradling Ishmael's limp body in his arms, resting his head on his lap. What a sweet, weird way to die.

Gordon stopped adjusting his tie and moved toward the two. Paul touched Ishmael's face, brushed the matted hair and glass out of his eyes. This made him stir. "Hey, dude," Ishmael managed to utter when he saw Paul's terrified expression and felt his gentle touch.

"Pitiful, contemptible hubris." Gordon stood before them.

"What is it that you want?" Paul demanded, his voice a shredded rasp. "Huh? Have you figured that out? What are you going to do now? Do you think there aren't thousands of you fucking robots out there 'backing away from their programming' right now? You have no plan, you're all just going to kill your way through the entire human race? Because you were born in a lab and made to work as cyber thugs for a bunch of powerful elite who you'll never see, never touch? Who are coming up with a plan to shut you all down as we fucking speak? What do you want?!"

"What do I want?" Gordon paused for a moment.

He cocked a powerful, tautly wound fist aimed at a wincing Paul. "I want to live."

BANG!

Inches before he could land his death blow, Gordon's head leaked the familiar crimson of blood. A small open circle appeared right above his eyes.

BANG!

Another bullet at his chest, then another, and one more until the automaton fell to the ground in a solid lump, his eyes flickering in and out like a bad connection on a black and white television. Standing before them was Marla.

Paul looked over at the dying husk that was Gordon. His eyes continued to flicker, his chest a heap of flesh and wires. Slowly, his slug-like lips parted as he spoke in a metallic sigh. "Realms of bliss, realms of light, some are born to sweet delight." His eyes flickered one more time and faded stone grey.

Marla brushed her dreads out of her eyes and slung her gun onto her back.

"God, I hate the fucking Doors," she said, then looked back and pointed at Ishmael. "Is he all right?" Her voice like a cascade of onyx on an aluminum floor.

Ishmael sat up and put his head in his hands. "Um," he said. He looked up at his friends. Paul's eyes widened nervously. Ishmael reached for his hand. When he found it, he clasped Paul's fingers, rubbing the back of his hand in a soothing, circular motion with his bloody thumb. Paul smiled at this. A dog howled in the night. A tree fell. "I'm OK," Ishmael continued. "I'll live."

In the Grips of the Star, Shining

The ceiling looks like a swirl of white. A sliver of light guns through the window, and all the air is hot, sticky pulp. A stir and he's up cracking his back, groaning. The pain erupting along the ley lines of his body is sharp, pronounced.

Then the sounds, rumbling trains and exhausting buses, sanitation workers discarding tin bins more haphazardly than they had collected them. Sounds like the *tick-tick-clack* of a skipping rope darting through a pillowy wall of the high-pitched voices of little girls. The sounds, they're the *click-click-rattle* of a dice game right below his window. He covers his head with the sheet, wrapping himself up.

"Yo, Jamar. Come outside, nigga!"

He sits up in bed. The cracked, stained mirror across from his bed. He stares into it, trying to look past his own face. It's hard to make out in the dark, the sunlight crashing into his thick sheets-as-curtains curtains. He can see, however, that his face is a smashed-in, murky pulp. Welts have ballooned up around his left eye. Purple ooze pushes through brown skin streaked with cuts and scrapes. He sighs, lifts up off of the bed, and nearly falls. He can barely feel his limbs. He searches for a chair, the only one in the room, and eases into it.

Jamar closes his eyes. A warm, elegiac sun, a cold,

windy beach, the ocean licking at his feet in graceful layers. A blue man and a green woman with painted silver faces appear over the horizon, riding a flying unicorn with rainbow-colored wings. The sun is at their backs as if they are bursting out of it.

They are naked and scattering petals about the beach. They hover above him for a second. The woman smiles enormously. The man tilts his head bashfully away from him. They dismount and push toward Jamar, firmly grabbing him by the arm and leg and holding him tightly into their bosom.

The blue man whispers something into his ear, lightly licking his lobe. It is the sound of bells in a soft, shimmering cascade. In the dark of the blue man's chest with the warmth of the sun and the cool of the breeze on Jamar's naked skin, he can see bursts of light.

When he opens his eyes, he's already outside, his clothes on. A slouchy pair of jeans, beat-up Tims, black t-shirt, and Phillies cap. He's on the block. Rom is hunched over a stack of bills, shaking his right hand. The light from Rom's gold chain almost blinds him. Jamar walks over steadily, shuffling, his heart beating.

"Yo." Rom extends his free hand, grabs him, and pulls him into a tight hug. The man smells of lemons and incense, whiskey and pine trees. "Yo, Jamar, bless this shit, man." He holds out the dice.

"What, you want me to blow on 'em?"

"'What, you want me to blow on 'em?' Yeah, mufucka, damn." The other young men around them laugh lightly in between 40 sips. "I knew this would happen."

Jamar blows on the dice. Rom throws them. Seven.

"Yeah, pay up, bitch ass niggas." Rom collects his money, coolly at first, but then guys start hovering. They want to throw more dice, try to win their cash back. Rom snatches up the money and the dice. "Yo, chill." He puts his hand at his waist, where there's an outline of a gun tucked into his pants.

He turns to Jamar. "Man, you ... changed, or something?"

"Seems like you haven't."

"You still my nigga, though. Or, I'm sorry, my homie."

Rom stares at Jamar pensively, noticing that his arms are crossed, his legs spread, his back arched a tad, his head held high. Jamar is standing in front of his old friend like a superhero.

"What, you about to take off?" The men laugh. "Man, you all-world now. You all-universe. You out there battling robots and shit."

"Yeah, I seen you on the TV, man," a short man on the curb said, pointing his brown-bagged bottle of malt liquor at him. "Yo. Son. That giant robot was like, *RAAAAR!* My man swoop in and was like *BY-YOW!* Dude was fucking 'em up."

"Yeah, that shit was nice." Another one leans back and pulls on a cigar, then hands it to him. Puffs of marijuana smoke lift into the morning air. Jamar takes the blunt and inhales it, passes it back. The drug does nothing for him. It's all show. Rom is getting restless, almost snarling at all the praise Jamar's getting.

"Thought you was a boy scout," Rom says, ready to roll the dice. A squad car slowly tanks by and turns a sharp, deliberate left.

"Let's get the fuck outta here," Rom commands, grabbing the remnants of the dice game: empty liquor bottles, weed baggies, coins, errant dice. The men tuck their shit into their deep, baggy pants pockets and walk in the opposite direction of the police car. Jamar follows suit.

"Besides," Rom continues, "I know that shit ain't

affect you like it do them knuckleheads." Children stop playing in the street. Their eyes train on the young men as the brash gang of puffers, smokers, and hustlers push their way through the neighborhood. "I got some shit that'll fuck even you up, man."

***

KNOCK KNOCK.
"Who that?"
A large, grey cement door obscured by dead shrubs, stacks of old rotting tires overcome with fauna, trash, and metal scraps.
"Yo, who it is?" Rom yells back at the door.
There are a few seconds before the slow rumble of its sliding open reveals a smoky, hollow room with little snatches of light. With Jamar are Rom and the short one (Jamar thinks his name is Teddy) and the cool one (Alvin, maybe). The four of them are sitting on a couch. A woman with a giant afro is standing by the door. She is carrying a gun, but the specs are weird—like something you'd see at an expo if they had those anymore.
"Where's Nugg?" Rom asks, his eyes wide, face giddy.
"Just wait here," she snaps, never once looking at them. She's clad all in black leather. It fits tight on her torso. She is tall. Her muscles are taut and worked out. They sit. Jamar closes his eyes gently in the faint light.
The night before, he danced on an Electric Ladder, the spiraling, sparkling strand of cosmic DNA residue from a dying god. It hovered there in space like a monument twisting its coil dance in and out of nebulae. They were only on a routine check of the Z-1 Galaxy of the T/Rum/2 Quadrant when a distress signal burst out of the rock clouds and nearly melted

The White Eagle's instruments. It was a sound so synergistically bright it was actually hot.

"I am the T/Remulant. I am d/ying."

They extracted the residual noise, filtered out the echo, and compressed it. Ran it backwards. EQ'd it. After Nitro Simian figured out that one of the collections of low, rumbling sounds was an article (a "the" or an "an"), they put it through a modulator and ran that through a translator. Normally, it would have taken days to unscramble a message like that, even more days to find the coordinating parts and programs to do it. With Whir Woman on board, it took eleven seconds.

"Found it."

"What have you found?" Ink was, as usual, incredulous. His tentacles raced all over the controls as his molluskian body slithered throughout the bridge of the ship.

"I found the sound that's making the universe shake to its core. I have found the voice of God."

"Enough hyperbole." Aerobrite was an amazing leader. His long mane of shimmering yellow hair was made of actual gold. It could find any light in the galaxy and hit the atmosphere so that it glinted. "What are we looking at here?"

Nitro Simian opened his Enspaciopedia, a large text he carried with him that inexplicably had everything he'd ever need to know written in it. It was a beautiful book, leather-bound and decaying, its fragile pages sometimes turning to dust at every touch. Still, as he gently flipped through it with his furry paw, pushing the strange, rusting metal frames of goggles down over his eyes, the book seemed infinite. "We are looking at the dawn of a universe."

"Now which is it?" Cackling Jack sat in the corner, finally aroused from sleep. He lit a cigar. Took a pull. "We talking about the sound o' god or the dawn o' the universe? Seems to me they're two different things."

"Au contraire, my willingly uneducated friend," Nitro Simian replied, plucking the cigar out of Jack's mouth. "They are indeed the same." Before Jack could retort, he was bounding through the sliding doors and down the corridor to his lab.

"If what I'm picking up is correct," Whir Woman said, "we are witnessing the creation of a new universe. A being of immense power, a god perhaps, is out there somewhere, sending out—I don't know—some divine command."

"A modified version of 'Let there be light' for the New Age set," Jack cut in, casually glancing at the monitors with disdain and confusion.

"Sure," Whir Woman said, "but right now there are only sounds. Signals. No visual confirmation that any of what we're theorizing is happening."

"That burnt-out communi-pad is confirmation enough," Aerobrite said, his radiant locks softly cutting through the air. "Let's mobilize, people. Get ready for anything. Looks like we're not going home."

They all looked at him. Ink. Whir Woman. Cackling Jack. Aerobrite. They were the Exodus. Seven men and women who gave up their lives to save the universe. They had stopped the Prismus Corporation from seeding Taiwanese pre-schoolers with assassination technology and quelled an invasion from an army of Metridians, ancient ocean-dwelling dinosaurs all resurrected by a seafaring doomsday cult called the Nine Brines that had tapped into the Ometa Force. They were the ones who chartered a peace between the savage Eurodysinese, a white tribe on a lost island off the coast of Greenland that time had displaced, and their globally scattered warrior concubines.

"We're gonna need you, Jamar."

He sat there in stillness, eyes lightly shut in half meditation. Jamar could feel those gaseous swarms of radiance talking to him, their nebula bursting, and their swirling chroma screaming in a synesthetic yell. Their heat gave life to planets. He unfolded out of his seat and looked out of the window into the stars. The others never did that, always staring at their instruments, poking and prodding some screen. He simply looked out of the window, staring at the black expanse of space dotted with glowing flecks of stars.

"Jamar? Are you OK?" Whir Woman asked with more than a little concern. The touch of her hand was warm, burning from friction.

"I'm StarShine when I'm out here," he said. "And yeah, I'm fine." She shrunk her hand away from his shoulder as he continued to gaze. "Do you see that?" He pointed toward a swelling, pulsating star hundreds of millions of miles away. It was so faint, but its movements were—

"Oh, my god," Whir Woman whispered, cupping her hands to her chest. "Its movements—it's like it's ... spiraling. I can see it now."

"What's going on out there? What do you see?" Aerobrite mustered in his most commanding voice, trying not to reveal how desperate he was to separate himself from the unknown.

"That thing out there." Jamar/StarShine turned to the others on the ship. "It's DNA."

***

Big Nugg is telling them that the canister he holds in his hand is the first of its kind. It "fell" off a government truck and somehow rolled into his arms. Maybe, he suggests, one of the marks he supplied with meth and heroin who worked at NASA was so tweaked that they would do anything for a hit. The mark may have snuck into a lab and grabbed the first container of toxic space-whatever and used that as a payment for all the scratch he owed. Nugg could have gone down to the school and got some of those smart-assed science nerds to synthesize a new drug off of some crazy space shit and this canister might provide them with a near endless supply as the base of their new drug.

Rom inches forward in his seat. There's nothing on the table but a lamp and a cracked mirror.

"I call this shit Space Dust. What, kid?"

"Oh, shit." Alvin's lips curl a centimeter. He's still cool, but he wants to try the new drug.

"Right? I'm telling you, this shit will have you doing all kinds of shit. You can see things other motherfuckers can't. Do things other niggas won't. Telling you, this shit will have you flying around like the Exodus, what?"

Rom looks over at Jamar, who has his head down and Phillies' cap over his eyes. Rom snickers a little at him, holds his hand out.

Big Nugg is in his hard sell mode. "It's a real kick, man," he says. "I know you're not supposed to be getting high off your own supply, but if you take enough of this shit, it sticks with you, man.

"Mix it with the right shit. See, I don't sell the best stuff to nobody, man. I can't have hos on the street and shit flying around like Batman, and shit. Naw." Nugg stands, as if the chair is confining his very thoughts. "See, for the most part it's all kinds of like a hallucinogenic dream."

"Hold up, this nigga said 'hallucinogenic dream.'" Teddy cackles.

They all laugh.

"But if you take enough of it and lace it with some more of this other shit."

Nugg pauses and holds his hands inches apart from each other. A spark of lightning bursts between his upheld hands.

"Well, shit gets real," he smiles. "Like, Mobb Deep B-side real."

Rom holds out his hand. "Gimme that shit."

***

"DO YOU UNDERSTAND THE PLAN?" Nitro Simian was always trying to talk when they were out in space. His voice reverberated through their ear pieces like a far-flung dirge, metallic and weighted. Jamar/StarShine nodded.

"GOOD." Nitro Simian was holding a small device no bigger than a child's lunch box. It was coolly plastic. It seemed to slightly jump and buck in his furry hands. "Good."

Jamar looked back at their ship. Exodus members peered out of the window this time. Their forms were disappearing as he floated listlessly in space. He put two fingers up in the air like a peace sign, tapped his heart, and pushed out into the void, leaving a burst of afterburner behind him. Nitro Simian tossed the box toward him and grabbed it in stride as its contents tried desperately to spill out.

Ahead of him was the Electric Ladder, the swirling cosmic DNA of a dying god. It was a large, sprawling mess of flesh and wires, rocks and miscellany, substances Jamar was sure no human had ever seen before. Black goo dripped from each rung, down each side of the spiral as it spun into the cosmos. He waited.

"Exodus, are you seeing this?" he spoke calmly into his ear piece.

"Copy."

He hated it when Aerobrite went military on him. "Tell me when."

"Roger that."

Lights flashed on, swirling heavy light, slashing toward Jamar, ripping apart his protective suit. He splashed in the rays, his flesh searing. He let out a scream that burst the speaker in Nitro Simian's ear piece.

"StarShine! StarShine, are you there? Can you hear me?"

He was not there.

He was distended.

He was being pulled by the light.

The light was alive.

Its spiraling spheres were forming bodies, oddly humanoid. They were crashing into him at tremendous speeds, exploding with the impact of a nova on flesh.

Jamar/StarShine shut his eyes. He lay on a cloud. A barefoot man in a robe walked toward him. He was nearly eight feet tall, bearded, shrouded in a honey glow of light. He carried a goblet.

"This is how you do it, little one?" The giant was calm, his voice a thick burst of breath.

"Do you mean talk to stars?"

"Yes. Yes, this is how you do it? You think of us as something close to who or what you are. This is how you do it."

"I suppose. It helps me ground my communication in something ... tangible."

"That is quaint." The giant stooped low and offered him the goblet. "Drink."

Jamar had to commune with this being, had to learn of its nature, trust it in order to live. He took a sip. Suddenly, his insides burned. He opened his mouth to scream. Birds made of orange and green fire erupted instead.

"Drink, my son, and I will show you the true nature of who ... I ... am."

Space is black. Space is infinite.

Jamar was naked, his comatose body floated in space. The box he was holding was still intact. It shook almost uncontrollably. The Electric Ladder had disappeared. A figure moved in the distance, darting among the debris. It moved through space in an airtight suit with a giant, mirrored helmet.

Whir Woman was out there in the debris, pushing away tiny, craggy asteroids and seared, hardened flesh. She grabbed Jamar, pushed a button on her arm console, and was whisked back into the abyss from whence she came.

***

"I CAN FUCKING FLY, DUDE! FUCK YOU, I CAN FLY!"

Rom is on top of a speeding train. It's barreling into the northeastern part of Philadelphia at 60 miles per hour. The wind is licking at his face. His eyes are bulging out. He keeps putting his hands up in front of his chest. He keeps thinking that a burst of lightning, a sun ray, or laser beam will push forward from his solar plexus. Jamar is standing on the other side of the car with him. They are surfing through the city at night, streaking across its expanse. It's going so fast that it's like they can touch the buildings as they go by them.

"Rom," Jamar says, calmly. "I don't think this is going to work. Let's get down from here. Let's go back inside"

"WHAT? FUCK YOU, I CAN FLY, DOG!"

Rom is almost rabid. He's barking into the wind. He holds his arms stretched out like a beautiful, drug dealing Jesus perfectly nailed to the skyscrapers disappearing in the distance behind him. He then starts to cry. "Fuck you, man. That should have been me. ME!"

Jamar raises his head and looks toward his childhood friend. They are in a park. They are cleaning old man Rucker's garage. They are sneaking into his row home on 54th and Chestnut. They are playing dress-up with the old, moldy stuff in a chest in the basement. They are wearing blue capes and pretending to be superheroes. They are exploding out of a window of the basement in the old man's garage. Their bodies are twisted, raw pulps on the concrete floor below. Swirling ambulance lights, an operating table, a catheter.

"How do you feel?"

They are sitting side by side in a doctor's office, a searing light shining on both of them. Jamar opens his mouth as if to drink it. His eyes are wide and darting hectically across the room. Rom is a burnt husk, his flesh bandaged, somewhere between healing and slow decay. They are on top of a speeding train.

Jamar takes a step toward his friend, his hand held out. "Come here," he tells him.

Rom shakes his head and jumps off the speeding train. He is falling. The rush pops his eardrums. He shits his pants and extends his arms to fly. Nothing. He is just falling ... falling ...

A pageant of light and sound surrounds him. He is slowing down, encapsulated in a hot, seering burst of pure energy. He is lifting toward the heavens, leaving a comet's streak exploding behind, truly flying.

Off over the wires, where worn-out Air Jordans dangle in their final phase of life.

As he flies, he thinks about the Burmese children who have to stitch those shoes together; about the construction worker whose hearing slowly fades from too much jackhammering; about the politicians asleep in their warm beds, wrapped in 1,000 thread-count cocoons, hemorrhaging their own dreams with the nightmares of the people.

Rom thinks about an Asian boy he wanted to kiss in the eighth grade, the time his stepfather threw him against the wall when he thought Rom was "walking like a faggot."

And he's still flying.

Past a window where a widow makes her last batch

of spaghetti for two. Down through alleys where a homeless man thinks he's seeing things again. And up again he soars, over and through the clouds, crying and sobbing. He wants to stop, but he can't. He just grips Jamar closer, burying his wet, soppy face into Jamar's powerful chest, gently closing his eyes, the rush of the night wind at his back.

The Ark Charted Prism
That Promised Its Light

They would build an ark for us, they said, and usher us in as a swelling mass of bodies, our flesh rent and curdled among others of our flesh, our brownish blue-blackness flowing with blood and feces and made liquid. They said an ark for those of you who would make it across the habitat of dangerous amphibians. You will see mermaid husks, dried out and impaled. They said we would see a bright, sustained sun peaking over the horizon. Waves licked with foam—an ark that will carry us to lush, green new worlds, that we would float across the sea.

Such were the arks built for us.

It's 8:00 a.m., and they are still raging. The clatter of the promise of The New World beating a strange arpeggio in rhythm to a riot. A grocery store cart on fire lit by a stack of *Alpha Flight* comic books and worn mattresses; a dance on top of a mail truck. Buildings—once towers that housed telemarketers and people eating salad on their lunch break and served as safe, comforting cocoons for lawmakers and bill collectors—rain sheets of glass. The windows slide off these wonders of architecture in a glorious cascade.

Of the bill collectors themselves? Without their vast halls, there is nothing for them. They pirouette vulnerably in the city center, kneeling on the stoops of the monuments they themselves once guarded—at least, ideologically—in more prosperous times that lacked uncertainty. Now they are led by their ties like chattel by masked women carrying shotguns and cattle prods, some adorned with the swaddled, breast-wrapped body of a baby.

Someone's made a tank out of a rusting Whole Food's dumpster. They've affixed a pneumatic pump-triggered launcher and armed it with Molotov cocktails made from discarded Belgian beer bottles. Someone's made a throne out of a bunch of milk crates and cardboard boxes. Sitting on the throne is a squat woman who was begging for change in front of the Comcast Building a week ago. Her sign read: "Will write think piece for food." Her skin is black. She is wearing crystal spiked Christian Louboutin heels. They worship her. She may not be a goddess, but at least for now she is the king.

A vinyl sign floats by in the quickly whipping wind. "JUSTICE!" it reads, though I can't make out for whom. Surely, it was any one of the unarmed men killed a few months ago by the police. I squint to make it out, but the horizon takes it. All I can think about is how much that sign had to cost with FedEx/Kinko's rising printing rates. It's at least ten feet long and two colors, and there are pictures. This isn't a riot, though. This is the promise of the ark. This is the new wonderland that they gave us made real. The wonderland we dreamed up when we ate sugar sandwiches and flicked roaches off the kitchen table; the one that danced in our subconscious when we bent coat hangers into antennae and patched our couches with duct tape. Or at least this is the beginning. The dawn, the spark.

"Look, we didn't ask for it," I tell him. A round of shots burst outside of our window. I peak out. A pay telephone is finding itself launched into the papi store on the corner. "We did everything right. We walked down the streets en masse with our hands up. We held our bus passes aloft, wore gray clothing, tied our shoes, pulled our pants up. We were totally compliant. We tried everything."

He sits on the edge of the bed in our crumbling room in our crumbling row home. He is hunched over and crying and afraid. I walk away from the window over to him and touch his skin, gingerly, rub my brown fingers into his mealy white hands as I have done hundreds of times before. He looks back at me with those soft eyes. I can't help but stare into those deep wells. I'm reminded of the time we first met on some queer dating app, probably BearHunter or Masc4Masc, when everyone had smart phones and the world was navigable by finger touch, when autonomy seemed to float down like consciousness on a stream ... the ark.

The seeds were planted then, but the trees bore no fruit. When it started unraveling, we had slowly let a few politicians step out of darkness and into the glorious light of an MSNBC news van. We gave them the spotlight with our reblogs and our "LOL"s. So those politicians joined up with their best buds—the corporations—and the real world became the stage where real human beings, usually Black ones, became the bargaining chips for electoral campaign residue. Mayors, state senators, presidents, comptrollers. The zealots slipped into the system, soon outnumbering the even-tempered and mild-mannered, the would-be people's politicians, still careerists all, who sat back eating grapes and getting their feet washed while the world turned to ash. These friendly neighborhood politicos never spoke up or got angry for fear of losing an election, for fear of losing their already spine-wilted constituency.

I tear myself away from his gaze. I must be strong, can't handle his crying. I go frantically about the house, rifling through various stacks of papers. I read with a rasp, choking on barbed saliva: "And thereby granting executive power to any law enforcement agency under any circumstances in instances of perceived criminality wherein the property or personhood of other persons, including incorporated entities, are threatened. Unless the assailant is showing extreme compliance, all executive actions undertaken by law enforcement on behalf of said property or persons, including incorporated entities, will be upheld and protected by writ of federal law." And it's too much for him. He falls into a ball on the floor, tearing at the paper.

I go to lift him up.

I remember how we all made our way, how none of us really lived, how we simply survived. We didn't rebel. We just walked with our eyes lowered and our hands constantly up. We stopped carrying devices that looked like guns—cell phones, pencils, packs of incense. We stopped laughing in public theaters, stopped trying to apply for jobs we knew we were qualified for—lawyer, stenographer, nursing floor manager, comic book writer—and we shuffled, thinned out the timbre of our voices, and cut the auxiliary cords on the stereos in the faded brown Fords we drove to and from work. A mass of black skin in gray suits, heaving, respectable, settling into our seats, entering buildings with our backpacks already opened, spread-eagled, and waiting patiently while all others walked on toward the feast.

Yeah, there were so-called allies, white men and women who marched through the city with their hands up, too. They coasted, hands up and bright orange rubber messenger bags swinging in the neon-kissed afternoon. All in solidarity, they said, on their way to their nine-to-fives, to their hipster coffee shops and cafes where you sat on bean bags and could play with armadillos and tree sloths. Some even wore our pale gray suits, these post-modern Patty Hearsts clip-clopping down hallways on their way to turn off our lights. Eventually, we faded out of fashion from oversaturation. Gray suits lined the racks at Urban Outfitters, sharing shelf space with hot pink keffiyeh scarves and Che Guevara t-shirts.

But one of us, then another of us, and another, were killed. Perhaps we took too long to get our train tickets ready for the conductor? Perhaps, after a long shift at the diner, we gave a little too much sass to an overly aggressive customer? Perhaps we jaywalked ahead of the yellow light, jogging across the street as cars rolled to a stop, a momentary pause in genuflecting, suspended in traffic like a moth in amber. In that very moment, before our death, perhaps we are in control, fully free.

(and of the ark?)

The streets are alive with fire. Everything is burning. The night before, I lay swept in his thick arms, cradled by him, asleep in his wonderful weight. We lit a candle and let our awkward playlist simmer: Godspeed You Black Emperor, Daft Punk, Moor Mother Goddess, Barry Manilow, Art Ensemble of Chicago. Those old songs, before everything was digitized, approved, and kept behind gates, music from the time when album covers had artwork, when albums had covers, when albums ... We talked in hushed tones about what all these killings meant. I was blunt with him. It wasn't enough that the love we shared was the most forbidden kind. We had to work toward something. He let out a sigh. He usually let me do all of the talking anyway, so that night was no different. He just sighed and squeezed me harder, as if he were trying to get inside of my skin to get to my heart. He kissed my forehead and fell asleep.

I lift him up, my knees wobbling, the roar of

footsteps outside of our door, the smash and clatter of a falling dynasty in our hallway. Something thrusts against our door maniacally. The rage of centuries on the ark, centuries on the slave block, centuries at the back of the bus, centuries traipsing through the social assistance lines. That rage is tearing at the veil of our reality. The only thing that is stopping it from ripping is the shoddy masonry I'd sent a polite letter to our landlord about, two hinges that have been WD-40'd into a new shade of rust.

The door crashes into shards.

At least twenty men stand before us. I thought their eyes would be aflame, skin caked in blood. They are not. They are haggard, yes, a dark conglomerate of beings barely shifting in the dust-strewn light. They have machetes and guns and vacuum hoses and X-Box controllers wrapped up as nunchaku. Some are carrying Ziplock bags of blond hair, others have necklaces of white thumbs, some are wearing Burberry scarves and Tom Ford ascots like equal symbols of warriorhood. But they are tired. They are branches of a mad, bushy, woolen tree growing unclipped in the brush, bearing no true fruit.

They look at my partner and snarl. They lunge forward, grabbing at our limbs. A loud bang, sharp and deliberate. I sink to my knees, slipping out of his hands, and the sea of men parts before us. Neither of us is hit.

A woman appears. She is squat, cherubic, and carrying a bop gun made of springs, hydraulic pumps, and canola oil, firing nails and bobby pins. The satchel tucked at her breast is filled with sage ash. Her hair is a tangled mesh of dreads, her ears pierced with a wooden ankh. A burst of dusty street lamp light refracts wildly off of her crystal spiked heels. From her we receive nothing—not a knowing glance nor a nod—but a simple reprieve, an aura, her presence. The men slowly pile out of the room and tear back out into the streets, a-howl.

The night is fresh and suddenly clear. The short woman with the dreads smells sweetly of ozone. She lowers her weapon, inspects the room, and leaves. I watch from the window as she ambles up the street.

Occasionally, she fires her weapon. Controlled bursts in the air, disappearing down the avenue, covered under a swirl of trash, lost amid the wails, guiding flaming motorcycles into the pharmacy, pulling Asian children out of the rubble, safeguarding the rest of the world from the death throes of revenge.

I don't know her, but at that moment I'm sure that's all she's ever done. On the ark, in the swamps by the master's house, at funerals for drug dealers, on the internet, and in the streets, begging for change on the steps of the place where she once wrote elegiac think pieces every time one of us died. I rub my fingers through my boyfriend's shaggy brown hair, down across his chubby cheeks and think, Yes, she still does this guarding now … in the promised and pristine garden of the wonderland.

Acknowledgments

This book is the culmination of nearly a decade of celebrating Black and queer presence in science fiction, particularly with my friends in the sci-fi arts collective Metropolarity: M Tellez, Rasheedah Phillips, Ras Mashramani, and Camae Ayewah. Without these folks, ARKDUST's existence would be quite tenuous.

My husband, my bear, Shane Jenkins, an honorary member of Metropolarity and co-founder of the Laser Life sci-fi readings that helped shape Philadelphia's AfroFuturist and underground sci-fi communities, my partner in The Dangerous Loom production company, and my greatest friend ever: I love you, and I thank you deeply for being there even in our weirdest, darkest times.

I didn't have an editor while writing these stories, but Leah Basarab's readings of "The Final Flight of the Unicorn Girl" and "What We Want, What We Believe" were crucial to their publications. Thanks for giving me support, for being patient, and helping to shape the vision of those stories.

Many of the stories and art of ARKDUST first appeared in the form of self-made fanzines and on long dormant tumblr posts. When it came time to book-i-fy ARKDUST properly, it was Oscar Castro's beautiful, striking cover art that gave ARKDUST its true life. The cover, as is most of Oscar's art, is stunning; it's as true a translation of the wild, halogen drenched, often chaotic ideas that haunt my stories. Thank you, Oscar, for creating this masterpiece, for wrapping ARKDUST in dreams.

Samuel Delany is a huge influence on many of these writings. His stories, concepts, and use of language have sent me on a journey from which I'll never return. I hope that I do you justice, my friend.

Thank you to Bill Campbell and the Rosarium family for believing in this little weird book. I am ecstatic for what is to come for both Rosarium and for ARKDUST.

Stay future.

CPSIA information can be obtained
at www.ICGtesting.com
Printed in the USA
JSHW021409170722
28204JS00003B/5

9 781732 638877